# THE WEEKEND

# THE
# WEEKEND

Helen Zahavi

Donald I. Fine, Inc.
New York

Copyright © 1991 by Helen Zahavi

All rights reserved, including the right of reproduction in whole or in part in any form. Published in the United States of America by Donald I. Fine, Inc. and in Canada by General Publishing Company Limited.

Library of Congress Cataloging-in-Publication Data

Zahavi, Helen.
   The weekend / Helen Zahavi.
      p.   cm.
   ISBN 1-55611-241-6
   I. Title.
   PR6076.A44W44   1991       90-56057
   823'.914—dc20              CIP

Manufactured in the United States of America

10 9 8 7 6 5 4 3 2 1

# CHAPTER ONE

This is the story of Bella, who woke up one morning and realised she'd had enough.

She's no-one special. England's full of wounded people. Quietly choking. Shrieking softly so the neighbours won't hear. You must have seen them. You've probably passed them. You've certainly stepped on them. Too many people have had enough. It's nothing new. It's what you do about it that really counts.

She could have done the decent thing. She could have done what decent people do. She could have filled her gently rounded belly with barbiturates, or flung herself, with gay abandon, from the top of a tower block. They would have thought it sad, but not unseemly. Alas, poor Bella, they would have said, as they shovelled what remained of her into the waiting earth. She must have had enough, they would have said. At least she had the decency to do the decent thing.

But pain and Bella made poor companions. She ran from pain, and thought it wouldn't find her. She shut her eyes, and held her breath, and hoped that pain would pass her by. The very thought of slicing into pale, translucent skin, or laying down her nubile form on the London–Brighton line, or hanging from the ceiling, with a flex around her

1

neck (is she not elegant, fragrant, pendant?) was enough to make her sphincter almost lose its cunning.

Pain, in short, was not her cup of tea.

There might have been another reason why she couldn't do the deed. Another reason why she carried on, regardless. Perhaps it was the thought of having been, and gone, and left no mark. The thought that if she finished it, she would have had no story. The thought that no-one even knew her name. For though she barely was alive, she wanted them to know her name. She wanted them, if nothing else, at least to know her name.

Some people are good at life, and some are bad. Bella was bad. No-one had taught her how to do it, so she stumbled along in the dark. She went crashing into taste, and tripping over refinement, and knocking her head against the brick wall of success and everlasting happiness.

She wasn't very good at playing the game, but she'd learnt to be a good loser. Losing seemed to suit her. It was something familiar, like an ache that's always there, but you know you'll miss it if it ever goes. The wonder is it didn't make her bitter. But it didn't.

All she wanted was to be left alone, which didn't seem a lot to ask. She expected little, and received less, and thanked her gods for what she got.

She'd found herself a tiny space, and you wouldn't begrudge her that. She'd carved out a space, in a basement flat, in a road that ran down to the sea. She sweltered in the summer, and shivered in the winter, and spent her evenings searching for damp, and it was a dull, grey life, a mutant kind of life, an abortion of a life. But it was hers, and she accepted it.

And nothing would have changed, no-one would have known her name, but for the man who watched her. An ordinary man, who watched her from his window. A man who watched and wanted, as he stood there at his window. He saw her in her basement, and had to have a go. He didn't have the sense to let her be.

2

He thought she was an empty vessel that he alone could fill. He thought he'd take her by the hair and pull her through the street. He thought he'd clamp a hand across her mouth, and bend her into what he wanted. His trouble was he thought too much. A little mind with big ideas.

For Bella couldn't bend.

As he found out, as she found out, Bella could only break.

# CHAPTER TWO

And now, the sketching in, the padding out, of what had gone before, of what it was that made her do the things she found she did.

(The juicy bits, the rank and lurid juicy bits, the bits that will make mothers warn their errant, toddler sons: Behave, or the Bella will get you – *those* bits come later.)

It began that summer, a hot and sticky summer that made the air shimmer and the walls melt. The beach was thick with tourists, while scabrous daytrippers thronged the pier, and language students clogged the streets, walking slowly as they ate fast food. Brighton beckoned to one and all.

Her basement was a dark basement. An unusually deep and dark basement. She drew back the curtain on the kitchen window, and the light seeped in where it could. Even then it wasn't enough to read by, not even during the day. Even during the day she'd have to sit under a yellow bulb if she wanted to read, which she often did.

She was a great reader. A great one for reading. Her favourites were the freesheets that she found on the doormat. She liked to read the small ads, to see what life might have to offer. There was a whole world out there, and surprisingly, comfortingly, it didn't seem all that much better than her own. Not quite as bad, but not much better.

One day in June, when the tulips on the shelf were beginning to wilt, and the corners of her mouth were beginning to droop, she folded up the paper and pushed back her chair and stood at the window and looked up at the sky.

You couldn't see much sky. Just a small blue square trapped between the houses. Not much sky at all, and Bella needed to see the sky. She had eyes that needed light and space. Enjoying neither, they were beginning to fail. She noticed it most when she was out on the street, and she realised that things were getting more blurred. Almost daily, almost hourly, they were getting more blurred.

It makes you feel sort of detached, when you don't see things clearly. When you don't see things as they are, but only get an impression of how they are. When you can't read people any more. You can't read their expressions, because you can't even see their expressions. So you have to get really close to them, and who wants to get that close to anyone, anyway?

She looked up at the patch of sky, and then she scanned the backs of the houses opposite, the ones that backed on to the back of hers. All of the houses were chopped up into flats, and some of the flats were chopped up into bedsits. A floating, transient population lived there. Students, drifters, dreamers. Some who were just passing through, and some who were there for the duration. Some who would be moving on, and some for whom Brighton was the end of the road.

She let her glance flick idly around, taking in the roofs, and the washing-draped fire escapes, and the grime that seemed ground into the brickwork. The windows grey with dust and gently undulating in the heat haze. Everything slightly seedy and slightly soiled.

A sudden movement caught her eye. There was a black

shape, directly opposite, framed in the second-floor window. The shape lifted a hand and moved it slowly from side to side. It was a bulky, masculine shape. A man in black. Looking out of his window and down into hers. Watching her from his window.

She waited for him to do what strangers do, when their eyes lock unexpectedly. She waited for him to glance away, or move away. To shrug and smile and look embarrassed. But he didn't move away, or turn away, or grin and look abashed.

He just kept watching her. And it was as though he was glad she'd noticed him. As though he wanted her to notice him. As though he'd been watching her before, and it was time that she noticed him.

She stepped back and drew the curtain across the window. She drew the curtain and shut him out, and with him the light.

You know the way some people go through life, telling themselves that everything's fine, everything's cool, everything's moving forward, and they're happy, happy people? Even when they're not? Even when they're stunted people with stunted lives?

You've seen them in the street sometimes, anonymous in the street. They stand on the corner and begin to frown as a shaft of cold clarity almost pierces them. They almost see how things really are. And then someone they know drives past and hoots and waves, and the frown dissolves, and they're no longer alone, and they're happy again. They grin at the receding car, and they carry on grinning as they carry on walking. That stupid, demented grin, you must have seen it. That idiot grin of gratitude.

She should have been like them. It's good if you're like them. It's good if you can get through the day and outlast the night by letting the lies help you along.

But Bella must have sinned in a previous incarnation.

6

She must have done something bad, and so she had to be punished. She was born with something missing. A vital part that an angel bit off and spat away, before she had a chance to bunch up her baby fist and grasp it. She saw herself as she was, and she saw her life as it was, and if she opened her mouth for a word of comfort, the truth came tripping off her tongue.

It's not so great being Bella. No bed of roses. No lotus life. No joy. And now there was the man in black, and she couldn't tell herself it was coincidence, she couldn't tell herself it didn't matter. Because it wasn't, and it did.

One August morning, she sat at the kitchen table, and ate warm toast, and drank hot coffee, and slowly read the second of the week's freesheets. A stripe of sunlight fell across the floor and climbed the wall behind her. She twisted her hair into a knot and tied it on top of her head. Her hand brushed the back of her neck. The skin felt moist.

Another hot and airless day, and she stood by the draining board and opened the window as wide as it went. Dirty dishes filled the sink, and the dried-up remains of her dinner. She switched on the radio, and the classic hits of Southern Sound washed over her as the water ran. She smiled as she watched the suds heap up. She always smiles when she does the dishes. Maybe it's the music, and maybe it's the movement, but there's something soothing about doing the dishes.

She was still smiling when she glanced up and saw him. A green shirt, this time. A man of many shirts. A multicoloured man. A man of subtle colour schemes. She couldn't make out his features. Not with weak eyes, like her eyes. She still saw only his pale, round face. The face of a man who kept out of the sun. She pulled the curtain across the window, and blocked out the man who shrank from the sun.

It feels strange when you close your curtain first thing in

7

the morning. Not quite right, somehow. Rather unnatural. Especially if you live in the basement, and you need all the light you can get. Things are getting bad, if you have to cover your basement windows. Things are closing in, if you live in a basement, and you shut out the light.

That's how she was beginning to feel. She was beginning to feel a bit closed in.

She kept the curtain drawn after that. It didn't really matter. Not really. You get used to anything, anyway. She knew that. She'd learnt that. She left the curtain drawn, not that it really bothered her. But she kept the windows shut, just in case. And she fitted window-locks, just in case.

Bella slept fitfully that summer. It's meant to be a languid time, the summer. A time of letting go and spreading out, of loosening up and lying back. Other people's summers. Not Bella's summer. Bella's summer was a sweaty summer. A tightened, clammy, cloistered summer. Closed, shuttered, barred. She was inside, doing time. An indefinite sentence with no promise of remission.

Bella is a light sleeper these days. It's difficult to sleep with her windows shut. Fresh breezes don't billow through your dreams, when your windows are shut. One of Bella's problems is that her life lacks breezes.

She locks her windows, and breathes stale air all night. This is what the Bellas of the world do. They lock their windows, and breathe stale air.

It makes them crazy, though. Just a little. Just enough to gnaw at them. A sort of trapped, animal feeling that creeps up on them at four in the morning, when the sky begins to lighten, and their heads begin to ache, and their limbs feel heavy, and their blood is sluggish from lack of oxygen.

Putrid air and bars. Men riot over less.


It wasn't so bad when autumn came. When autumn came it wasn't so bad. Winter follows autumn, and in winter they all huddle at home with their windows shut. She'd be like everyone else, come the winter. So it wasn't so bad.

One evening, in November, she thought she'd have some cocoa. It seemed a sort of autumn thing to do. She heated up the milk in a fairly stainless pan. The phone began to ring, as now and then it did. She put the gas on simmer, and leaned across, and picked it up.

"Hello?" she said. Politely.

Milk bubbled softly in the background.

"Hello?"

A click, and the line went dead.

She replaced the receiver. She took a mug from the cupboard, and spooned in cocoa powder, and poured the milk on top, stirring slowly.

The phone rang again. She took a hurried sip, and answered on the fourth ring. The cocoa was so hot that it scalded her tongue.

"Yes?" she said. Demanded, really.

He didn't answer straight away. He took his time. She'd have to wait before she heard her master's voice.

"Why do you keep the curtain drawn?"

He had an accentless way of speaking. You couldn't place him from the way he spoke. He gave nothing away when he spoke.

She glanced at the shrouded window. Was he watching from across the gardens?

"That's right," he said. "I'm watching you."

Her tongue was swelling in her mouth.

"It took a while to find your number."

"It's not listed."

"I know." He paused. "You passed me in the street."

"Did I?"

"The other day."

"That's nice," she said.

"You might have said hello."

"I'm sorry?"

"I said you didn't even say hello."

"My eyesight's not too good."

9

"So get a pair of glasses."

"I will," she said. "You're right. I will."

Her tongue began to throb.

"There's something I've been meaning to tell you," he said.

She leaned across and turned off the gas, to stop the pan from burning.

"I don't really know how to put it," he said, "but I think you ought to know."

She couldn't bear it when he paused. To hear him speak was bad enough, but to hear him pause was worse.

"I can see you through the curtains."

"I'm afraid I don't . . . "

"I can watch you moving through the curtains. You must have got them from the market. I don't like cheap curtains. Cheap women buy cheap curtains."

And in the island of silence that follows, she wants to say that they're not hers, she's a tenant, they're not her curtains, not her choice, don't call her cheap, please don't call her cheap.

"I can see the shape of you through the material. When you have the light on I can see you moving about. I like the way you move. I like looking down and seeing you move and knowing you're in there. I can tell by the way you move that you know I'm watching you. You've got a kind of look-at-me way of moving. It's naughty of you, to move like that, when you know I'm watching."

Bella in the basement.

"I don't know what you want," she said. A small and hopeless lie. She hears the sound of her voice. Such a high, weak, apologetic voice. A child's voice. An infant's voice.

"Ask not what I want from you. Ask rather what you can get from me. I don't take. I give. I'm a very giving person. I'm going to give you what you deserve."

"If you call again, I'll report you."

"Only if I call again? You're enjoying it this time, then. I

10

knew you would. I knew you'd enjoy it. I know what you'd enjoy. I want you to stand in front of the light, facing the wall, so you're in profile. Then I want you to touch yourself. I want you to do that for me now, and then I want— "

She slammed down the phone. She slammed down the phone and slumped in the chair and felt the fear churning and the nausea rising. She held her head in her hands and opened her mouth and wailed soundlessly in the empty room.

Bella in the basement.

Is she pathetic? Does her weakness repel you? Does the thought of her huge, demented, victim's eyes turn your stomach? Don't judge her. Don't judge her unless you've been there.

She took the phone off the hook and switched off the light and stood by the sink in the dark. It took a while for the shaking to stop. You shake with fear. It's not just a phrase. Your limbs start to jerk, like a marionette. She stood by the sink and shook in the dark.

The following night, he phoned again. She knew it was him. She answered the call, though she knew it was him. She heard the voice come down the line.

"You shouldn't have put the phone down. That was bad manners. I don't like bad manners. Bad manners make me angry. If you do it again, I'll have to punish you. Do you understand?"

Does she understand? She's always understood.

"Do you?"

"Yes."

"Say you're sorry."

Bella in the basement.

"Say it."

"I'm sorry."

She said it like she really meant it, because she really did. Bella was truly sorry. She was sorry she'd put the phone down. She was sorry she'd picked the phone up. She was sorry she'd offended him. She was sorry for being Bella.

11

"That's better," he said. "Be a good girl."

Bella in the basement. Bella buried in the basement. And he's running his nail along her coffin. He's scratching the wood of her coffin. He's tapping on the lid of her coffin, because she might be buried, but she's not quite dead.

"I dreamt of you last night. Did you dream of me?"

He didn't breathe heavily. He didn't pant with suppressed excitement. His voice stayed flat. Almost monotonous. Totally controlled. He sounded normal. He didn't sound like he should have sounded.

"Did you dream of me?"

"No."

"Don't lie. I don't like liars. You did dream of me, didn't you?"

"Yes."

"What did I do to you in your dream?"

"I don't know."

"I know what I did in your dream. The same as I did in mine. Ask me what I did. Ask me nicely. Ask me nicely what I did, or I'll have to punish you."

"What did you do in your dream?"

"Nicely."

"Please . . . "

The sound of him sucking in breath before he began.

"I climbed through your window one night. I came through your window and into your bedroom. I stood by your bed and watched you sleeping. I was there beside you as you slept. You opened your eyes and saw me. You wanted to scream, so I covered your mouth. You bit my hand, so I hit your face. I took hold of your hair, and pulled you out of bed. I filled up the bath, and washed you clean. Then I rubbed you dry, and oiled your skin."

Bella in the basement.

"I like smooth skin."

She wrapped the flex around her fingers. Round and round and round her fingers.

"And then I fucked you on the floor. I fucked you hard

12

on the bathroom floor. I pushed it in until you puked, and you loved it, you loathed it, you'd better believe it."

He sighed softly.

"That's what I did in my dream."

She pulled the flex tight.

"If you tell anyone, you'll be sorry. Remember that."

He cut the connection.

# CHAPTER THREE

Pain wasn't really her thing. Her ability to tolerate it was unusually low. She didn't need it, like some people need it. She didn't want to cause it, and she didn't want to suffer it.

She thought you could live a life without pain. It was a flaw in her character. A weakness. She thought if you didn't hurt other people, they wouldn't hurt you. She thought you could be gentle in the jungle.

She knew nothing. She really knew nothing.

After that night, the night she entered his dreams and he entered hers, she stopped answering the phone. She kept the window locked, and the door bolted, and the curtains drawn and she stopped answering the phone.

Autumn turned to winter, and the sea turned from aquamarine to granite grey. By February, Brighton had been through hail and sleet and snow, and if she had to go out she wore her imitation sheepskin boots with rubber soles that gripped the ground.

Sometimes she used to sit on the bench in Brunswick Square. It lost most of its trees in the great gale of '87, but it's still an elegant square. Apart from the flies, and apart from the dogs. The houses are Regency, with soaring columns and wide balconies. You can look from the sea to the houses and back again, and it's so calming that sometimes you feel like you almost belong.

She went to sit there one afternoon. It was unseasonally mild. Watery sunlight fell on her face, and turned the snow into slush. After the first twenty minutes she began to feel contented, in as much as she ever felt that way. You can sit there for hours. If you don't bother anyone, they won't bother you, but you might nod at those you've noticed once or twice before. She liked to sit in the square. She kept her curtains drawn, so she liked to sit in the square. She'd look up at the sky and shut her eyes and bathe in light. That's all she did, when she sat in the square.

Something wrong with that? Something abnormal? Is she taking too much? Is she too grasping? Is she gobbling up altogether too much?

She just used to sit in the square. She just used to sit in the sun, in the square. And nothing would have changed. She wouldn't have changed, and Brighton wouldn't have changed. Nothing would have changed, if he hadn't seen her that afternoon, and sat down beside her in Brunswick Square.

He was wearing an overcoat. The black of the sweater made a V beneath his neck. It was strange being that close to him, when she'd only seen him at a distance, across two gardens. When she'd only heard his voice across the wire. Now he was so close she could see everything. The blackheads around his nose. The sediment at the corners of his eyes. The way his lips had a bluish tinge.

"Here we are, then," he said.

She smelt mint when he spoke. People with bad breath often suck mints. They ruin their teeth, but they don't offend.

"You look tired," he said. "You're not taking care of yourself."

15

She stared at the sea. She didn't want to move from the bench. If she moved from the bench, she couldn't sit there again. Brunswick Square would be his square.

"Nice day," he said. "Bit cold."

He looked younger than he'd sounded. He looked clean, brushed, barbered. A wholesome-looking young man. A credit to his mummy.

"I've missed talking to you," he said. "I quite enjoyed our conversations."

He was healthier than the blur she'd seen in the summer. Short days must suit him. He had roses in his cheeks. He was peaches and cream, a young girl's dream.

"I read something in the paper, once," he said. He leaned slightly towards her. "Something a bit peculiar, if you follow my drift."

He spread his legs out in front of him. Sand-coloured desert boots.

"This girl was walking down the road. Minding her own business, so to speak. She was just walking down the road. Middle of the day, I think it was. A side road, not a main road, but there must have been people about. She was walking down the road, when a car pulled up and they dragged her inside."

His mintiness on her face.

"She wasn't on the game, or anything. Not like some."

And he turned and watched her profile, which he hadn't been able to watch for a while.

"They just grabbed her and pulled her inside. Then off they went. She was yelling, the paper said."

He chuckled quietly. You could barely hear it, but his whole body shook. The whole bench shook.

"They pushed her down on the floor, and turned up the stereo. Drove to a lock-up somewhere. Out she came. Slapped her around a bit. Slapped her around a bit more. Then two of them did their stuff. You know the sort of thing, of course you do."

Of course she does.

16

"But the third one, he wasn't interested. He just waited till they'd finished, and you know what he did?"

She's looking at the grass. The grass needs cutting. They should cut the grass in Brunswick Square.

"I said, d'you know what he did?"

She shook her head.

"What he did," he continued, "what he did was he pissed in her face."

And he reached out a hand and cupped her chin and turned her towards him.

"Now fair's fair," he said, "I'm no prude," he said, "but that's what I call out of order."

You know what they say about showing icy contempt? You know what they say about grace under pressure? Keeping your integrity? Preserving your human dignity?

It's fantasy.

You try being icily contemptuous when you're being buggered by a Turkish police chief. You just try it. Nice theory, but it doesn't work. You just try making with the dignity when you're being violated. When they're in your mouth. When they're bigger than you, and stronger than you, and they know it, and you know it, and the ground lurches beneath your feet, it really lurches beneath your feet, and if you had a God you'd ask him why he'd forsaken you.

Bella knows it. Bella's always known it. Bella knows that she's never really had any rights. Rights are fiction. Rights don't exist. You can't touch them. You can't taste them. You can't see them. You can't smell them. They're not there. They don't exist.

You only have what you can defend, and if you can't defend it you don't have it. Bella can't defend herself, so she can't belong to herself. Bella belongs to no-one and to everyone. She is everyman's. She is the original collective. To each according to his needs. Let them all drink from her well.

She watched the gulls wheeling and diving above the

sea. She should have been a seagull. She could have been up there above the waves, dipping and skimming above the waves. She could have dropped her droppings on his head, if she'd been a seagull.

He took her thin wrist in his thick fingers. She tried to pull away, but he held her tight. She tried to twist away, but he held her tight. And he liked it. She could tell he liked it. The more she struggled, the more he liked it.

Small women look stupid when they struggle with big men. There's something about their weakness. Something about their vulnerability. Like when you see a policeman leading someone away in a headlock, and whatever you think of the copper, whatever you think of the blue-eyed boy in blue, there's still something contemptible in the sight of the prisoner being walked along the pavement. Bent over and led along.

The next time you see it, think of Bella. Bella's had her head in an armlock all her life. She's been pulled by the hair all her life. They've been frogmarching her along all her life.

He encircled her thin wrist with his thick fingers.

"You ought to learn self-defence."

"Leave me alone."

"You shouldn't keep the curtain drawn."

"I want you to leave me alone."

"You're not being friendly."

"Please don't do this."

"I haven't done anything. I'm just making conversation."

He held her wrist in his fingers. He turned the hand over and looked at her palm.

"You've got small hands. I didn't realise you had such small hands."

He pressed into her palm with his thumb. She felt the nail dig into her skin, and felt the skin begin to break. It's nothing new. She's the kind of woman men dig into. She's the kind of woman who gets dug up. A very ploughed, forked, trowelled kind of woman.

18

"I could break your hand," he said. "Your hand looks very breakable. I could do it now. Your hand would break. You'd have a broken hand."

He pressed the hand to his lips and kissed it.

"The funny thing," he said, "the strange and peculiar thing," he said, "is that you're not my type. You're not what I would call an attractive woman. You're not the sort of woman who attracts me. Nothing personal, but there you are."

He smiled.

"If you don't mind my saying so."

But Bella doesn't mind. Bella never minds. Bella sits and listens as they speak. She lets them dribble in her ear. She lets them press and nearly break her hand. She lets them tell her if they want her as a woman.

She lets them, because she has to let them. Because her bones, as they can see, are very brittle bones. You wouldn't have to press too hard to break her bones. So don't look at her and think she doesn't know. Don't think she doesn't know she has to let them.

"I want to hurt you, but I don't know why. Tell me why I want to hurt you."

"I don't know why."

"You must know why."

"I don't," she said. "I'm sorry."

"I'll come and see you soon and make you sorrier."

Bella on the bench in Brunswick Square. Taking the air in Brunswick Square. Hunched on a bench in Brunswick Square. Bella Nobody, in Brunswick Square.

He pulled a magazine from his pocket.

"There's a photo that's been bothering me."

She looked down at the folded-back page. It showed a woman on all fours. She wore a leash around her neck, but nothing else. She smiled over her shoulder at the camera.

"Do you think she looks like you?"

"No."

"I think she looks like you."

"She's not me."

"She's a slutbitch."

"Not me."

"A manhole."

"But she's not me."

"You're all the same."

"Leave me alone."

"Slags and scrubbers."

"Please leave me alone."

"Tarts and whores who give it away."

"Just leave me alone."

"Like you're Oxfam, the way you give it away. Feed the starving, the way you give it away. You think you're special?"

"No."

"You think you're someone?"

"I'm no-one."

"Don't get big ideas."

His finger pointed at the open slit.

"That's all you are."

A middle-aged woman was walking her dog. She nodded at Bella and her nice young man.

"Please don't do this."

"You make me do it. You're leading me on. You're just a pricktease leading me on. A dirty little sow who's leading me on."

He rolled up the magazine.

"You know what I'm going to do?"

"Tell me what you're going to do."

"I'm going to hurt you. If you tell the police, I'll kill you. But if you don't, I'll only hurt you. It'll happen soon. I'll come into your home and I'll hurt you. I want you to imagine what I'm going to do. I want you to picture in your mind the different ways I can give you pain. Think of the worst thing I can do to you, and think of me doing it."

And then he went. He stood up, and tucked the magazine into his pocket, and pulled on a pair of brown leather gloves, and turned up his collar against a non-existent wind, and winked at her, and said he'd be seeing her, and walked away.

She sat on the bench and watched him go.

Does she matter, this Bella-person? This nothing-person? She doesn't think so. She doesn't think she matters. That's what she thinks, at this moment, on the bench in Brunswick Square.

She thinks of what he'll do to her. She thinks of all the different ways he's going to give her pain. She pictures the worst he can do to her, and then she pictures him doing it.

How can she matter, this Bella, this nothing-Bella, this rubbish-Bella, this Bella who sits and listens?

He never touched her again. He didn't have to touch her. They both knew he'd already forced his way inside. He'd already violated her space and set up camp. Squatter's rights. Possession is nine tenths of the law, and he already possessed her. All she could do was to crouch in a corner, and wait for the day he would come through her window.

And so it might have continued. Pathetic and slightly boring if you're not involved yourself. An everyday story of urban blight: the fall and fall of Bella, whose only claim to fame was her total and consuming insignificance. The worm-like, irrelevant Bella. Less than nobody.

But fate can be strange. Fate can be fickle. Fate can be wandering by one day. Aloof, uninterested, kicking a tin can along the promenade. Nothing to do because it's all been ordained. And fate can suddenly stop, and stare, and almost smile.

Fate found Bella one night. Fate came to her by moonlight and whispered in her ear.

And when she woke up, she knew she'd had enough.

# CHAPTER FOUR

This is the day her story starts. What went before, the way she sat and waited, the way she let him watch her, was just the prologue. What went before was all preamble. This is where her story really starts.

It was gone three, when she got to the North Laines. It's the part of town you go to if you want your head shrunk, or your palm read, or your destiny revealed. It's the mystic, altruistic part of town. It's where they take you by the hand, and lead you through your dreams.

She trawled the side roads until she found what she wanted. A small piece of paper had been stuck to the inside of a window. She bent down and read the message:

IRANIAN CLAIRVOYANCE SERVICES
Unlock your Hidden Powers
The Key is Within

She went down into the well of the basement, and stepped over a bin bag, and rapped on the door. The sound of a chair being scraped back and footsteps coming into the hall. A guarded voice came from behind the panelling.

"Who is it?"

"Bella."

"Do I know you?"

"Not yet."

"What do you want?"

"I want the key."

The door opened and she stepped inside and looked up into a gaunt and pallid face.

"My name is Nimrod," he said, extending a limp hand in greeting. "Welcome to my subterranean abode." And he ushered her, with oriental grace, into a tiny sitting room.

He pointed to a velvet cushion on the floor.

"Please be seated."

His lips moved in what she took to be a smile.

"It is a consultation you intended?"

"It is," she said, watching as he moved about the room. A low-wattage bulb burned under a green shade. It gave the walls a bilious tinge.

"Why the curtains in daytime?" His windows were shrouded with heavy drapes. She knew the syndrome.

"My eyes are too sensitive," he said. "They cannot take the light. The light is too bright. I prefer the night."

"Are you a poet?"

"Versification is certainly one of my gifts. Perception is obviously one of yours." He had a bony, beautiful, ravaged face, and was dressed in black, like a Sixties playwright. "Do you take tea?"

"I do."

"The English like tea," he said. "And the Persians like tea."

He pulled thoughtfully on his moustache.

"Nation shall speak unto nation."

He stepped through the bead curtain which hid the kitchenette. She heard water splash into a kettle, and the hiss of gas before it flamed.

He came back into the room.

"It takes a while."

He picked up a scarlet cushion from the corner, and pummelled it into the shape he wanted.

"How can I help you?" He placed the cushion carefully on the floor.

"Tell me what will happen."

"That I cannot do."

"What can you do?"

"I can help you change." He sat down and crossed his legs and stared at her, like a starved and cadaverous caliph.

"Who says I want to change?"

"You wouldn't be here if you didn't." He placed his hands on his knees. "Why are you here?"

"I want to change."

"Into a different person?"

"Yes."

"A better person?"

"No."

"What, then?"

She watched a purple vein begin to throb in his temple.

"Cut out my heart and put a stone in its place. I want vengeance."

"Spoken like a Persian."

"Thank you."

He put his head to one side and listened as the water began to bubble.

"I like that sound," he said. "It's a comforting sound." His dark eyes looked wistful. "Hell must sound like water boiling. Only louder."

He stood up and swayed suddenly. His balance wasn't good. He didn't look a balanced man. "Tea is served."

She followed him into the kitchenette. There were no cupboards, only shelves heaped high with packets of rice and tinned tomatoes. She glanced down at the dark green lino on the kitchen floor. She couldn't remember the last time she'd seen lino. Even her GP had got rid of his lino. He turned off the gas and opened the lid and let steam billow

24

out of the samovar. He used his left hand. The right one was a withered stump of scar tissue. He glanced at her.

"I had a disobedient hand, so they punished it."

He hummed quietly to himself and poured brown liquid into china cups. "The tea is black, as you can see. Milk in tea is a heathen abomination."

"Have you been a clairvoyant long?"

He frowned at a damp patch on the wall.

"About a month," he said, handing her a cup and saucer.

"That's quite a long time," she said. "And before that?"

"Before that I cleaned the tables at McDonald's, and before that I worked on the pier, and before that I sold ice-cream with chocolate flakes in it, and before that I weeded people's gardens, and before that I was in hospital because of my nervous predicament, and before that I was in Pentonville waiting for my hearing, and before that I was in the hostel at Harmondsworth."

"And before that?"

"Before that," he said, "I was in Tehran. I ate apricots and figs," he said, "and roast lamb so tender it fell off the bone. I wrote for an English-language paper. Hence my rather superb command of your mother-tongue."

He took a small sip and followed her back into the sitting room. They put their cups on a low table, and rearranged themselves on the cushions.

"For you fully to appreciate the guidance I can extend," he said, "I should first expound the details of my own rich and varied life, the subtle nuances of my insights, the infinitely complex intricacies of my inner mind."

He paused and leaned forward and pushed a bowl of mixed nuts across the table.

"However, I am aware" – and his sigh seemed to well up from the depths of ancient Persia – "I am alas aware of the fundamentally fiscal nature of our relationship, the monetary rock against which we dash our sensibilities."

"You mean I have to pay you."

"Just so," he said. "My fee is seven pounds per hour.

Cash in sticky hand. Which is why I feel moved to deny you the full benefit of my wisdom, impecuniosity being one of the stronger impressions you convey. I shall limit myself, unprofessional though some might think it, purely to the analysis and resolution of your own specific trauma."

"Your way with the verbals is beginning to grate."

"It's an acquired taste. My mother considered me a genius."

"Were you an only child?"

"More or less." He blew into his cup. "I had four sisters."

He slowly sipped the hot liquid.

"We lived in North Tehran, in a villa of quite sublime beauty."

He drained the cup.

"Our sewage flowed out on to the slums below."

He dabbed at his lips with a paper napkin.

"Economists call it, I believe, the trickle-down effect."

He placed his cup on the saucer and held out his hand.

"One hour's consultation, though one hates to be vulgar."

She dropped a five-pound note and two coins into his open palm. He relaxed and leaned back on his cushions, noting the time on his watch.

"Now we begin." He placed a thin Turkish cigarette between his lips.

"How does this work?"

"You tell me things."

"What things?"

"Hidden things." He sent a cloud of blue smoke spiralling into the air. "Dark things."

"And then?"

"Then nothing. Then I listen. I listen to what you say. What you say and what you really mean."

"Sounds more like therapy than clairvoyance."

"Call it what you will. It's cheap at the price."

Bella took a deep breath. She inhaled to her limits. She filled her lungs with the syrup-sweet air of his incensed room. She cleared her mind of workaday thoughts, the

26

mundanities and profanities that were her lot. She blotted them out, banished them wholesale and without appeal to the Siberia of her psyche.

"My name," she began, "is Bella." And here she paused and saw his pallor and wondered if he ate his greens.

"I was born in 1963, the day they shot Kennedy."

"One era ended, another began."

"Precisely."

"A black day for humankind."

"So they say," she said.

He sucked heavily on the cigarette, and his cheeks collapsed into his face. He looked even more skeletal.

"And your parents?"

"My parents?"

"They who begat you," he clarified. "The begetters of Bella."

"They eat a lot of fruit, and they have no imagination, but they adore me, as one would expect. I am their baby. The living embodiment of their passion. Their guarantee of immortality."

She paused and filled her mouth with sweet liquid which clung thickly to her teeth.

"They live in the suburbs, and go to Devon twice a year, and read the *Daily Mail*, and never use the f-word."

"You sound critical."

"Who am I to criticise? They are mine and I am theirs. What they lacked in money, they made up for in kindness."

She placed a salted pistachio on the tip of her tongue.

"I would, of course, have preferred the money, but that is neither here nor there. Bella bears no grudges."

He shifted on his cushion.

"Is that it?"

"That's it."

"Could you perhaps give a fuller description?"

"That was the fuller description."

"Are there no siblings to travel with you through life?"

"Just the one," she said. "My older brother. He masturbated to music from an early age."

She watched his sudden interest with some confusion.

"Is that significant?"

"Musicality," he pronounced, "is always an asset."

"His rhythm was astounding."

"He sounds a remarkable fellow."

Nimrod stubbed out his cigarette on the rim of the saucer.

"And this was your family?"

"Apparently," she said. "The damp earth that nurtured me. The soil from which I sprang. Banal perhaps, but mine."

She picked up her cup and swallowed some black and tepid tea. She watched him rub the palm of his hand in a lazy, circular motion against his shin.

"And yourself, Bella. Therein lies the problem, I take it. What of yourself?"

"Myself," she said. "Myself has always been a great disappointment to me."

"Self-knowledge is often painful."

"So who needs it?"

"Indeed."

She began to pull loose threads from the carpet. He put a hand in his pocket and brought out a string of silver beads. He leant across to her.

"You flick them with your thumb," he said. "They're good for the nerves."

She held the beads in her left hand and pulled at the carpet with her right. "Where do I begin?"

"Begin where the pain began."

She flicked one of the beads back and forth.

"I went away to college when I was eighteen. Liberal Arts. A little bit of this, and a little bit of that. One of the tutors wore a black leather jacket and preached free love. He was very clever and very nasty and I adored him."

"How long did it last?"

"Not long. One night was all he wanted. The first night and the best night. Once he'd drawn blood he left. Didn't

28

want to know afterwards. A fortnight later I asked him why. 'Different men have different standards,' he said. 'I like to storm the ramparts, so lesser men can follow.' And then he smiled his charming smile, and said he wouldn't want to drink from a greasy cup."

Nimrod grunted. "Never trust an intellectual."

"I dropped out within the month. Not a wise move, perhaps, but squats welcomed me, anarchists fed me, men filled me. And no more free love: they paid to put their greasy spoons in my greasy cup."

"You don't look like a whore."

"I'm not a whore."

"In my country they shoot whores."

"In your country they shoot everyone."

"Why did you do it?"

"A girl has to eat."

"Why did you really do it?"

"I liked it when they gave me money."

"What did you charge?"

"Not enough. The profit on each deal was minimal. The cost, to me, enormous."

"You couldn't put your price up?"

"There's always others who'll do it cheaper. I had no bargaining power."

"Piecework was ever thus."

"But I did have Joey, my protector and defender, my teacher and tormentor. I was his best. He told me that. His best and his bravest."

"And he looked after you?"

"In his way. He gave me things. He gave me presents." She looked at the stump at the end of his arm. "I like presents."

"He had money, this Joey?"

"As much as we could make."

"He controlled you."

"Totally."

"And you let him."

29

"We all let him."

"You didn't have to."

"We had to."

"He was a parasite."

"So tell me something new."

"You could have left him. Formed a collective."

She sniffed. "We weren't communists."

"Did he sleep with you?"

She flicked the beads of her Persian rosary back and forth.

"He preferred women in a different line of work."

Nimrod formed his fingers into a steeple and nodded gravely. Had he possessed a goatee beard, he would have stroked it.

"So he didn't sleep with harlots," he said. "A man of principle."

"That's a cruel way of putting it."

"A spade must be called a spade."

"And a pimp a pimp."

He smiled at her. "The pimp is worse than the prostitute, the English say. What are your feelings about him now?"

"Mixed feelings. Bittersweet feelings. He had his temper and he had his tantrums, but he also had his tenderness. He could be very tender. You could go to him with any problem, and he'd try and sort it for you."

She fingered a small scar on her chin.

"But he didn't like lip. He couldn't stand lip. Lip was something he couldn't abide." Her face softened at the memory. "Nobody's perfect though, are they? And he was a lovely dresser."

She wasn't used to opening up like this. She wasn't one to analyse what she felt, in front of a man she didn't know, for a cash-in-hand fee. She looked at him curiously. He seemed strange and exotic and distant.

"Do you have many pimps in Iran?"

"They're running the place," he said. "But they don't have Joey's scruples. They don't have the scruples of a Joey. They don't have Joey's tenderness."

He gazed at the floor.

"They fucked the people, and left them bleeding on the battlefield."

He shrugged.

"Pardon my phraseology."

"Feel free."

He heaved himself up from his cushions.

"More tea?"

He fetched the samovar and placed it on a high table by the wall. Steam curled out when he lifted the lid.

"I think not," she said.

Wisps floated up from the cooling metal, and he poured himself another cup. He stepped softly back to his cushions. His feet were shoeless, sockless. He had naked Persian feet.

"Are you cold?" His thin frame shivered and he placed his hands around the cup to warm them.

"No," she said, the chill of the room eating into her bones.

"Why did you choose such a life?"

"It seemed a good idea at the time."

"You enjoyed it?"

"It had its moments."

"How many?"

"Two, perhaps."

"How did it finish?"

"One day he told me I'd let myself go. He said I'd become a bit raddled."

"What does raddled mean?"

"It means I'd become a bit of a mess."

She pulled a whole handful of threads from his carpet.

"He had a point. I wouldn't deny he had a point. But it was a bit abrupt, the way he did it. A bit sudden. One minute I'm his best, and the next I'm carrying all my worldlies down the Cromwell Road."

"Parting is such sweet sorrow."

"Too right," she said. "And he didn't even settle up. I tried to insist, but he said I was getting lippy."

31

Nimrod shivered again. He didn't seem at all well. "I think we'll switch on the other bar," he stretched across to the electric fire, "as there's two of us." They watched the lower bar glow first red, then orange.

"Then what?" he prompted.

"Then I just moved around."

"Around where?"

"Nowhere special. Just around."

"How did you live?"

"As best I could."

"You sold sex?"

"No," she said. "Poetically put, but no."

"I don't mean to offend. You have to peel off the layers to find what's underneath."

"There's nothing underneath."

"We'll see." He lit another cigarette, then leaned forward, holding the pack. "Excuse me for not offering you before."

She placed one of the cigarettes in her mouth, and let him light it. "My only vice," she said.

They smoked in silence for a while, listening to the sound of tobacco burning up. She didn't know why she'd told him what she'd told him. Even her mother didn't know what he now knew. Not that it mattered. He didn't matter and she didn't matter. They were two marginal people, living in basements, playing word-games to fill the time.

"I moved down here about three years ago," she continued, when the silence became too heavy. "I packed my bag and came down to Brighton."

"All roads lead to Brighton," he said. "That's why we're here, you and I. It's the end of the line."

"Do you like it here?"

"Sometimes."

"What do you like best?"

"It's not Tehran."

"And what do you think of England?"

"Too many foreigners."

32

"Like you?"

"Like you, my dear. Like you."

"It must feel odd, being a refugee."

"It feels odd," he said. "It feels odd and cold and damp and lonely."

"You need a woman."

"I need a woman."

"Any woman?"

"Any woman."

"Even a harlot?"

"Do they give credit?"

"I don't know," she said. "I'm out of touch."

"Are you offering?"

"I'm not a whore." She wound a strand of hair around her thumb. "Am I a whore?"

"You're not a whore. You're no longer a whore. You were once a whore, and are now in Brighton. I was once a journalist and am now in Brighton. Shall we continue with the story?"

"I've told you my story," she said. "My life, habibi. My life in your hands."

"Not yet the whole story. What happened to you? What happened to bring you to my door?"

"Nothing happened. Until a few months ago, nothing happened. I went into myself. I looked inside myself and there was nothing there, so I thought I'd camp in the empty space. Everything had drained away. All the hope and all the fight. Trickled away on the train down to Brighton."

"A delayed reaction to your previous life."

"You think so?"

"Self-hatred, my dear. I know it well."

"Is there a cure?"

"There's always a cure."

"It's not that simple."

"Everything's that simple."

The electric fire at full strength gave his face a healthier, if demonic, glow. She watched as two red sparks danced in his eyes, and wondered how he made ends meet.

"Are you on Social Security?" she asked.

"Does the sun shine?"

"Not on me, it doesn't."

"That's part of your problem."

"Tell me the solution, not the problem."

"The solution, like the key, is within."

"Very nice. You should write those messages in Christmas crackers."

"I have an application pending."

"Shall I continue?"

"Please."

"Someone's been threatening me. He says I'm a slut."

"How does he know?"

"He doesn't. He thinks all women are sluts."

"May his shameful part shrivel up."

"My neighbours avoid eye contact."

"They cannot gaze upon the truth," he said. "Few can. On the return to my homeland of the False Imam, piss be upon him, a voice visited me in the night, saying: Scribbler Nimrod! Thou art truly endowed with the seeing eye. Get thee away from this cesspit."

"So you left."

"Unfortunately, no. I dallied for a day. I dithered for a week. I postponed and prevaricated. I closed my eyes to mad mullahs, and my ears to the rancid rhythms of the mob. I waited too long, and then it was too late. Not only was I deaf and blind, but also stupid."

His bony shoulders sagged.

"When they give dung-collectors Kalashnikovs, it's time to get out."

He sighed sadly.

"Well, my dear. *Nil desperandum*, as they say in Baluchistan. Nimrod is here, and vengeance shall one day be his. As the saying goes: Have patience, and the body of your enemy will be carried past your door. But enough of

34

glorious imaginings. The candle burns down, and we must resolve your fate. More nuts?"

"Please."

"Tell me what else you feel."

"Flotsam and jetsam," she said. "The last in the race. Black clouds and no silver lining. Just another pebble on the beach. The last out of bed and the last in the queue. The last on anyone's list for anything. I feel lost and abandoned, last in life."

"The last shall be first," he said. "It is written."

"Is that your honest and unbiased opinion?"

"That is the sincere evaluation of Scribbler Nimrod. Late of the Tehran Press Club. Later still of the Evin Institute for Psychological Correction. Presently resident-in-exile of this excrescence on the south coast of your most hospitable country." He lit another cigarette. "Now tell me more. Tell me what frightens you."

"Everything frightens me."

"What above all?"

"Men," she said. "Men frighten me."

"You've known many men. You know their weakness. You know their cowardice. What is there to fear?"

"Their hunger frightens me. The way they look at me frightens me. What I read in their eyes frightens me."

"And what do you read?"

"What they want they must possess. What they can't possess they must penetrate. What they can't penetrate they must destroy."

"And what have you got against penetration," he asked, flicking ash into the saucer, "all of a sudden?"

She realised that he wasn't quite the lovable oriental loony he pretended to be. She looked at him for the first time with a kind of loathing.

"I know what I was," she said, "and I can't change it. I can't change it and I can't forget it. But it's the past. Another country. It's gone, and you can't bring it back."

"You're the one who won't let go of your past," he

35

said. "You're the one who needs it, and you're the one who feeds it."

"Easy for you to say."

"Easy to say and easy to prove. You've got no identity without it. You've got no excuses without it."

"That's a lie."

"They've used you, Bella. They've used you and abused you and thrown you away. All of them. All of the three-legs. They spread you out and entered you and pumped you dry."

"I don't have to take this."

"They've all been in there. They've had a good poke around. It didn't matter what they looked like. It didn't matter what they thought, or even if they thought. It didn't matter if they opened their mouths and a fart came out, you still had to smile like it was scent from heaven."

"I don't have to take this from a shitty refugee."

"You were open house, my dear. They only had to meet your price. Your remarkably low, remarkably value-for-money price. They paid their pound and in they went. And you let them all in. Anyone's money was good enough."

"Fucking foreigner."

"You let in all the lepers. All the retards. All the malforms. The stupid, the smelly, the whining and pathetic, the squat, the boring, the outrageously flatulent. You let them all in, and you licked off their slime, and you liked it."

"You piece of stateless scum."

"I'm a citizen of the world."

"They want to put you back in that nut-house."

"Do they really?"

"They want to chain you up and walk away."

"Doctor Bella, I presume."

"Only I don't see why my taxes should feed you."

"Tuppence doesn't go very far these days."

"You lousy, sneering, foreign creep."

"I try."

She suddenly felt hot. As if waves of heat were washing over her.

36

"Tell me what's in your head," he said.

"You don't want to know that."

"I want to know everything."

"I want to put my hands around your neck and squeeze until it snaps."

"Is that all?"

"I want to choke the air from your lungs."

"And then?"

"I want to watch the light die in your eyes."

He slipped his left hand inside his jacket. "There are people like you in the Lebanon . . . "

"I want to cut your head off."

" . . . mad-dog people . . . "

"I want to finish you."

" . . . suicide people . . . "

"I want to wipe you away."

" . . . they call themselves Hizbellah."

"I want to shut your mouth up once and for all."

"So what stops you?"

"Your strength stops me."

"I'm not strong."

"You're stronger than me. All men are stronger than me. Every filthy bloody foreigner that's washed up on the beach is stronger than me."

She was breathing hard. "Now you know."

"Now I know."

He took his hand out of the jacket. He was holding a slim and stubby steel bar. He pressed a button and a blade shot out.

She stared at the flick-knife in disbelief. "What are you doing?"

"Giving flesh to your secret fears."

"What fears?"

"You know the ones I mean. Being alone with a madman." He smiled a thin and mirthless smile. "Poor Bella."

He held the knife in front of her face. It glittered and shimmered in the soft light.

"Aren't you afraid I'll kill you?"

He put his thumb against the point of the blade and pressed down until a bubble of blood appeared.

"You wouldn't dare."

"You think not?"

His eyes narrowed and he leant across and a small sound escaped from her throat.

"Hold out your hand," he ordered. "Palm up."

Cold metal touched her skin. He held her hand in his, and closed her fingers around the shaft.

"Does it feel good?"

She touched the button, sending the blade swishing into the hilt and out again.

"Does it feel good?"

She held the knife in her hand.

"It feels good."

He released her and leaned back.

"You can keep it."

She looked down at the knife. Such a beautiful knife.

"You don't want it?"

"Your need is greater. Consider it a gift. I believe you said you like gifts."

"I'm grateful."

"So you should be."

"I didn't really mean those things I said."

"What things?"

"The insults. The sound and the fury."

"I think you did, but it doesn't matter."

She waited. He didn't elaborate. "Did you mean what you said about me?"

"That you were no holes barred?"

She nodded.

He shrugged with mock regret. "More or less."

She ran a finger along the edge of the blade.

"Tell me what to do. I need an answer."

"You hold the answer in your hand."

"I don't think I follow."

"I don't think you do."

"Explain it, then."

He passed her a cigarette, and took one for himself. The lighter he used was a throwaway lighter. A disposable lighter, for a disposable man.

"For most people," he said, "the world is divided into murderers, victims and spectators. Should they be given the choice, they can choose to be a spectator. They can stand on the sidelines and cheer or jeer. They can make fine moral judgements, and condemn the criminal, and praise the pious. They can keep their hands fairly clean, and their thoughts fairly pure, because they don't risk anything, and they won't lose anything. Are you with me so far?"

"So far so good."

"The problem, my dear, is that some people don't have those choices. People like you. Little people, Bella. Little people with big dreams. You don't have a choice because you're a lamb. You are what we call lamb-like. And when they see a lamb, even spectators sometimes want to be murderers. They see a lamb and they start to salivate. Lambs remind them how hungry they are. You are a walking temptation, Bella. You tempt them with your weakness."

"What can I do?"

"You must choose what you will be."

"I want to be a spectator."

"You don't have that option."

"So I have no choice."

"You have a choice."

"What choice?"

"The only choice."

She listened to the sound of his watch. She listened to his watch as it ticked through the seconds.

"I'm not a murderer."

"Murderer or victim. Take your pick."

"You might be wrong."

"I'm never wrong."

"I can't do it."

39

"You can."

"How do you know?"

"Because I know."

She looked at the knife in her hand. The blade glowed red from the electric fire. She held it tenderly in her hand. It felt so good. It seemed so right. She pressed the button and the blade flicked back. She shook her head from side to side. She was afraid. She was afraid of what would be done to her. She was afraid of what she would do.

"Take the knife," he urged. "Take the knife and take revenge."

"There's no other way?"

"None."

"The murderer or the victim?"

He nodded slowly.

"The butcher or the lamb."

# CHAPTER FIVE

It was Friday night. The weekend begins on Friday night. The good times begin on Friday night. She sat in her kitchen and sipped chilled vodka and waited for him to call.

She wanted him to call. She couldn't do it, if he didn't call. She needed him to make the move. She had to hear his murmur down the line. She had to hear him murmur darkly down the line. She couldn't find the courage, unless his voice came trickling down the line.

Later, much later, years later, two days later, she'd know you mustn't wait. Within two days, she would have learned that you mustn't wait too long before you do it. If you wait too long, you go under.

Women like her can't afford to wait. Brittle-boned women aren't built to absorb blows. You can't wait too long, if you're Bella. You've got no reserves, if you're Bella. No Queensberry Rules, if you're Bella. She'd learn that she had to strike first. Women like her have to do it and run. Women like her can't sit and wait. No-one will save them, if they just sit and wait.

But that was a lifetime later, at the very last moment of a very dirty weekend. On Friday night she was only beginning. Constraints still clung to her like dead skin. She still thought there were lines you didn't cross. She

41

still thought there were depths you shouldn't plumb. She still didn't know that all you can do is go out in the dark like a mad dog.

So she sat in her kitchen and waited. She sipped chilled vodka on Friday night, and waited for him to call.

She'd got through one third of the bottle by midnight. Stolichnaya vodka. She drank it with ice and lemon, smoking and waiting for him to call. Sitting, drinking, smoking and waiting. It's an odourless, flavourless, colourless drink, which she drinks not to forget, but to remember.

For the more she drinks, the clearer her head becomes, the more lucid her thoughts, the sharper her understanding. The more she drinks, the better she thinks.

She sat and drank and smoked and thought. She thought about Persia, and Pentonville, and exile, and two-bar electric fires. He'd been right, the refugee. The displaced person had got it right. Right was what he had been. He'd clarified things for her. He'd sorted them out in her mind, so that she could see the connections she was making and those she was missing.

He'd laid both hands on her head – his withered hand and his whole hand – and touched off something buried in her brain. He'd lifted her up and left her with a sense of possibility, a surge of sudden energy. He'd given her the key, and sent her away. Back to her basement to sit and to wait. To wait for the one with his foot on her face. To wait for the one who stood at the window, who lurked in the shadows and shrank from the sun.

She sat and smoked and drank and waited, and at five past two, as she sucked on the lemon she'd fished from the glass, having just emptied the ashtray for the third time, her feet encased in nylon slippers, her tongue like tobacco in her mouth, the phone began to ring.

She picked up the receiver. She waited for his voice.

"Hello," he said.

"Hello there," she said.

"Me again," he said.

"I know," she said, breathing back her vodka-breath.

"You sound relaxed," he said.

"I've been meditating."

"Where were you this afternoon?"

"Out and about."

"Doing what?"

"This and that."

"I think you're getting used to me."

"I think I am," she said. "In a sick sort of way."

Breezy little Bella. She could tell it disarmed him, the way she breezed at him. You don't expect a Bella to come breezing back at you.

"I don't know your name," she said.

She could put a face to his voice, but no name to his face. She wanted to know his name. She wanted to know his name, but nothing more. He didn't interest her. She didn't find him interesting. He was an irrelevance, who would shortly be an absence. He was an itch she needed to scratch. A boil she would have to lance. A bit-player in the drama she was going to enact. And spear-carriers, chorus-liners, bit-players are deeply boring when you're about to become a star.

"Tell me your name," she said.

She listened to the silence. It was a different kind of silence. Now it was her silence. She'd made the silence. She'd silenced him. One afternoon with a raving wreck of a refugee was all she needed to find the strength to silence him.

"Tim."

"Timothy?"

"Tim," he said. "My name's Tim."

"That's a sweet name."

The kitchen was heavy with smoke. It hung in blue-grey coils around her head. The kitchen was dense with smoke. She could have cut the smoke, it was so thick. She could have slashed it with Nimrod's flick-knife. She could have

43

sliced it down the middle. She could have stabbed it where it curled above the cooker.

"You sound different," he said.

"How different?"

"As if you think you matter."

"Don't I?"

"You know you don't. Any fool can see that you don't. I thought you understood that you don't. Even a backward bitch should know when she doesn't matter."

The clock on top of the fridge showed ten past two. It was a folding travel clock, the sort they used to make with a leather case.

"You don't think I'm worth much," she said.

"I don't think you're worth anything."

"But you do think of me."

"All the time."

"It's nice to know someone cares."

"If I didn't care, I wouldn't want to hurt you."

"You're repeating yourself."

"So what?"

"So it's boring."

"So too bad."

She could hear him breathing. She never used to hear him breathing. His breathing sounded a bit blocked up. Someone ought to drain his sinuses. Someone ought to drain away the snot he kept sniffing down his throat.

"Your phone bill must be on the large side."

"You'll be paying it," he said. "You're going to pay all my bills."

"I haven't got much cash."

"I collect in kind."

"I need more time."

"There's none left. This is the final demand. This is your red-letter bill. This time I'm coming round to collect."

"And if I won't pay?"

"It's like the gas and electric. If you don't pay up, something gets cut off."

"I think you've got a problem, Timothy."

"Tim."

"I think you've got a problem, Tim."

"I don't care what you think."

"I think you've got what's known as a psychosexual problem."

She saw his face in her mind as she spoke. She saw his tongue pass quickly over bloodless lips. Bella has begun to break the rules. Slowly, tentatively, one step at a time, Bella has begun to break every rule they ever made to keep her down.

"I'll be coming round to see you," he said.

"I think you're impotent."

"Shut your mouth."

"I think you can't do it."

"Shut your stupid mouth."

"You want to try stroking it."

"Dirty slutbitch."

"You want to try sucking it."

"I'm going to finish you."

"You want to try bribing it."

"Shut your fucking mouth."

"My mouth doesn't fuck," she said. "I don't have a mouth that fucks. I don't fuck with my mouth."

It must be tough if you're Tim. If you're an ordinary, honest-to-goodness, salt-of-the-earth sort of guy, who likes swilling beer with the boys, and swapping tales of random conquest. If you find a silent woman to feed your fantasy, and you stroke your heavy scrotum as you whisper dank obscenities down the line. If you trail her in the street, and you watch her shrivel up, and it makes you feel a man.

And you don't question it, you don't doubt it, you don't think twice about it. You've got a cock, and the cock is king.

Then suddenly, horribly, disgustingly, she opens her filthy mouth and she whispers filthy words. And it's not meant to be like this. You don't dream of it like this. You're

45

not even sure you want it, if it's going to be like this. The lousy bitch. The lousy, stinking, pricktease bitch, they're all the same.

Because you only want to hurt her, you only want to damage her, that's all you want to do. You want to crush her so completely that she'll never raise her head. You have to keep her down. To keep your foot on her face and her face on the ground. You've got to do it, to feel alive. The point of what you do, the basic point of what you do, is to help you feel alive. That's the way He made you, and that's the way you are. Not for you to question why. Blasphemy, to question why. That's the way you are.

"You know something," he said, "some people really wind me up."

"Do they really?"

"They really get me going."

"Is that a fact?"

"I mean they ask for it, they really ask for it."

"Yes?"

"And when they get it, they wonder why."

"I'm going to bed now."

"I haven't finished yet."

"Must dash."

"Don't put the phone down."

"It's been divine."

"I've got something to say to you."

"Another time, perhaps."

"Something I'm going to give you."

"You've got me a present?"

"Just for you."

"How kind."

"You'll be getting it soon."

"Can't wait."

"Guess what it is."

"I couldn't possibly."

"It comes in a bottle."

"I don't drink wine."

"You pour it on the skin."

"I buy my own perfume."

If she turned out the light, the clock would glow in the dark. It was like having a cat, the way it glowed green in the dark.

"Tell me what it is."

"You have to guess."

"The suspense is killing me."

He laughed softly.

"Speak," she said. "Speak now or forever hold your piece. What is it?"

She heard him suck in air.

"Acid."

The word was still bouncing around in her brain when the dialling tone began its whine.

She replaced the receiver in its cradle. She'd wanted to think a little more before she acted. Possibly brood a little more. Prepare herself a little more, before she did what she had to do.

But he'd phoned her. He'd touched her down the wire. He'd listened to what she said, and he'd listened to the way that she said it, and he'd ripped through the gossamer glibness and he'd reminded her of what they both knew. He'd reminded her that she was a lamb, and he'd made the final connection that decided it all. And now she really had no option, any more. She couldn't put it off any longer. Not even one more night. Like Nimrod said, she'd been given two choices. And she was left with the single, inescapable truth, that better the butcher than the lamb.

She went into the bathroom and flicked on the light and stood in front of the sink. She let the water run for a few moments before bending down and splashing her face. The water was ice cold and made her skin contract. She reached for the towel and dabbed her face dry and smoothed cream on her hands. Then she looked up and stared at herself in the mirror. Her reflection stared unblinkingly back at her.

47

An unforgiving face, with unforgiving, night-black eyes. Bitter-cold eyes, like the bitter-cold water.

She told Nimrod she had nothing inside her. She told him it had all drained away, and left a void she couldn't fill. She told him there was nothing there any more, and she believed it when she said it. But now she knew she'd been wrong. Now she knew that there was something there. Something rigid which had taken root.

She knew what it was when she looked at her eyes. She looked at her eyes and she felt it growing. A hard little nugget of rage was growing inside her womb.

It didn't take her long to dress. She pulled on thick ribbed tights, with socks on top, and heavy-duty denims, and a turtle-neck jumper. It felt strange to be dressing in the small hours. Indecent to be dressing in the small hours. She laced up ankle-high trainers and eased her hands into thin velvet gloves. God bless you, Bella. God bless you for reclaiming the night.

She hadn't eaten much that day. Her hunger would have to wait. Her food-hunger would have to wait. She slipped on the Swedish padded anorak she'd bought in Gloucester Road. She zipped it up to the neck, and wrapped a crimson scarf around her face.

She should have worn a balaclava. A balaclava would have been better. But balaclavas are made for the close-cropped head. They're made for the lads. Whoever they are. Wherever they are. Balaclavas are made for the boys.

But the boys in their balaclavas could not imagine Bella in her basement. Tooling up, pulling on gloves, zipping up the jacket. Bella in her basement is beyond their imagination. She's beyond belief. She's a video nasty in velvet gloves. Mad-dog Bella has slipped her leash.

She needed something to prise open the window. She needed something hard to get her through the window. She went on to the landing and pulled out a box and rummaged around until she found what she wanted.

The thick wooden shaft of the hammer fitted her palm

like it was always meant to be there. It was heavy in her hand. She liked to hold it in her hand. She liked its brutal heaviness in her hand. She liked to hold brutality in her hand.

She slipped it inside her jacket, and shut the cupboard door, and went into the kitchen, and stood in the dark in front of the window. She drew back the curtain, for the first time in weeks, and looked out into a blank and empty courtyard.

She stared out of the window and into the darkness. She thought of where she was about to go. She thought of what she was about to do. And tantalising images kept drifting through her mind. A seductively silent movie that spooled through her head in grainy black and white, but kept fading out before the climax.

There's no point in pre-empting. You can't guess how things will turn out. You just have to hold on and keep hoping. And she's very good at holding on. She's very good at hoping. A very patient little person, who used to wait and see what happened. But this time, it's different. This time she's going to happen to someone else. How does tonight differ from all other nights? Tonight is the first night that Bella will happen.

She felt her way through the darkened kitchen and up to the back door. Bending down, she slid back the bottom bolt, then reached up and pulled back the top one. She took the key from the nail in the larder, and put it in the lock, and turned it anticlockwise, and the door swung open. She stepped out, and pulled it to behind her.

The night air is a special kind of air. It's a clean kind of air. The petrol fumes have blown away, the traffic noise is muted. She climbed the steps, and stood in the garden, and breathed in the pure night air.

This is something new for Bella. This is a first for Bella. One small step for Bella, but a huge leap for womankind. She's never done this before. She's never drawn back the

49

bolt on her bolted back door, and climbed up the steps on a bleak winter's night.

She stood on the grass, with the stars shining down, and smiled to herself as she breathed in the air. The sweet night air, when all is still, and nothing stirs, and the law-abiding are in their beds.

# CHAPTER SIX

The earth was frozen beneath her feet. Hard, unyielding mother-earth, beneath her dainty feet. She crossed the patch of scrubby ground. A night-light glowed dimly down the terrace. A burning light to keep the bogeymen at bay.

She stood on a broken bath and peered over the top of the fence. His window was dark. A dark and restful rectangle. The sash hung a few inches above the sill. You lucky man. You lucky, lucky man, with your fearless, open, unlocked window that lets the air swirl in.

She heaved herself over the top and slid gently down the other side. She clambered over builders" rubble, and around a rusting pram, and ducked under an empty clothesline, and reached the fire escape. A sharp and moonless night, and the bitter wind stinging her face, and her breath condensing before her eyes, and the fear and the thrill and the joy as she gripped the iron railings.

She padded silently up to the second floor. She stood on the landing and stared at her house, hulking black against the grey sky. They say that travel broadens the mind. You get a different perspective when you move your position. You start to see things differently, when you stand on your neighbour's fire escape in the middle of a frozen

51

night. She looked back at her flat, and something inside her contracted.

She stared down at her kitchen window, as he had stared so many times, as if from a great height. Like watching a bird in a cage as it hopped about behind the bars and thought it was alive. She looked back at her basement. Back at where she'd come from.

A hole in the ground. A pit in the belly of the earth. And she's climbing out. The water's up to her chin and she's climbing out.

The sash lifted easily and without a sound. She pushed it halfway up and climbed through the gap and into his bathroom. When you're in someone's bathroom, it's like when you're in their kitchen. You breathe in their smell, and it seems to assault you, and you feel like an animal in another's den. The room reeked with his smells. His aftershave, and his soap on a rope, and the wet towel that hung off the radiator, and the talcum powder he powdered himself with, and his shaving foam, and his hair gel, and the spring-fresh substance he poured down the bowl. Such a clean man. Such a clean, perfumed, fastidious man.

She felt for the handle of the door and opened it and peered into a dim hallway. Yellow light from a streetlamp forced its way through a fanlight of frosted glass. She moved across the carpet and paused beside a door that was slightly ajar. She could hear him breathing in his bed. Heavy, rasping, mucoid breaths that made her want to slam the phone down.

She went back down the hall and into the lounge. After the packed earth, the carpet seemed to suck at her feet. She crossed the room and checked the curtains, then flicked on the floor-lamp and looked around.

And a very nice room it was, if you like that type of thing. Plants, tape player, prints on the wall. Interesting little designer knick-knacks on the shelves. Style magazines strewn on low tables. There was a single row of books.

Not a great reader, Timothy. Not one of the literati. Not a member of Brighton's rampant intelligentsia. She would have burnt them, had the Nazis not given book-burning a bad name.

She looked around the room. She wanted to foul it and defile it. Burn it down. Blow it up. Wipe it out. Lay it waste. She wanted to spray her name in gaudy letters all over his dove grey walls. She'd never understood the kids with the cans before. She'd never understood what drove them to make their mark in the only way they could. She looked at the walls and wanted to spray Bella Was Here in such a way that the B defaced his Parisian print. She wanted to spray her spoor all over his walls. She wanted to slash the sofa and smash the stereo, to rip the curtains and watch a dog defecate on the charcoal-coloured carpet.

She sighed regretfully. She is not a vandal. The violence of vandalism is alien to her nature. The wanton, mindless destruction of inanimate objects, the venting of passion on insensate matter, seems to her particularly perverse.

And her energy is not boundless. Bella does not brim with zest. Even now, even tonight, even with her new perspective on her own life and the lives of others, her energy is definitely finite, and she must not squander it. She carries what energy she has in a small yet brimming cup, and she must be careful lest she move too fast and it splashes over the rim and soaks away.

The light from the lounge spilled into the hallway and half-lit his bedroom. He lay sprawled out, limbs flung comfortably to the four corners. He didn't sleep the way she had slept, curled up into a tight little ball of foetal fear. She watched the sheet rising and falling, falling and rising, his head a dark shape against the pillow.

Here we are then, she thought. Here we are.

She moved closer. Her stomach was empty. She felt giddy with hunger, and giddy with hatred. She gazed down at the man. This whispering man. This whispering, threatening, slumbering man. This malevolent man, who'd blighted her life.

She stood by his bed. She'd entered his home, and she stood by his bed. And she was masked, and armed, and unafraid.

# CHAPTER SEVEN

His eyes were moving under their lids. She watched his eyes. They moved as he dreamed. He was dreaming of her, as he slept in his bed. He was dreaming of having her there on her floor. Having her hard on the bathroom floor. Pouring the liquid on to her skin. Hearing the hiss, and smelling the burn, and watching her melt on her bathroom floor. She shrieked in his dream, and she died in his dream, and his eyes kept moving under their lids.

She took out the hammer, and gazed at his face. Because of this man, she quaked in her burrow. Because of this man, she shut out the light. She gazed at the sleep-sodden face. That nothing face. That nobody face. That featureless deviant's face.

She held the hammer in her velvet glove. She raised her right arm. Just bring it down. Just bring it down, upon his head. Just swing it down. Just let it fall. Just do it now. Just do it, while you can.

But she couldn't. She couldn't do it as he slept. Whatever she is, she's not a monster. Nor a nutter. Nor psychotic. She's not yet cut the bond so completely that she can snuff him out in his sleep. For Bella is a nice girl. Sugar and spice, and all things nice. And when nice girls batter nasty boys,

55

they make sure to wake them first. Silly, perhaps. But there you are.

Timothy slept on. A blithe spirit, blithely oblivious to the sight that awaited him. The sight of Bella in his bedroom, with her hammer held high.

She half-closed her eyes, and put her finely-drawn lips to his ear. Her tongue darted out and licked the lobe. The cotton moved above his groin. She breathed hot breath on his face, and he smiled in his sleep, with her scent surrounding him.

Base, base Bella. Silken seductress. Necrophiliac nymph of the night. Destroyer of worlds.

The bastard looked so blissful. He could have had that bliss forever. He'd have been happy, and she'd have been happy. He could have lived his pointless life. He could have lived his natural span. He could have had threescore and ten, and smiled in his sleep as he dreamt dirty dreams. He could have kept it all inside his head. He could have done it in his head, the way most people do. He could have locked it up inside his head, and kept the world at bay.

But that wasn't enough. That wasn't enough for Timbo. He had to find a woman and press her with his clammy flesh. He had to reach inside his skull and pull out something putrefied and rub it in her face. A need he had. He couldn't help it. To feed the need was all he wanted.

And of all the women he could have chosen, of all the women who would have wilted, the fool had chosen her, whose needs were even blacker than his own.

She watched him as the sheet went damp. She watched him as the minutes passed. She'd won the game. She'd beaten him. She'd got inside his lair and stood beside his bed. Magnanimous in victory, she gave him a few fleeting moments of ecstasy, the ecstasy that can only come when Bella licks your lobe.

Had he known he was condemned, this would surely have been his last wish: to have this pleasure in the dark, to have this comfort in the dark, to climb the mountain in the dark and down the other side. All this she gave him, although he wasn't worth it.

But Bella gives, and Bella takes away.

After the party you have the reckoning. There's a time to come, and a time to go. A time for joy, and a time to be judged. The solemnity of the moment struck her. Had she gone in for ritual, she would have removed her crimson scarf and replaced it with a neat little square of black.

For Bella's justice is not biblical justice. She could never take an eye for an eye, and a tooth for a tooth. The weak and flaccid parity would make her nearly puke.

She wants an eye for a tooth, and a life for an eye.

And so, reluctant though she was to intrude, loth to gatecrash his private garden of delight, but aware, none the less, that *tempus* inexorably *fugit*, she held the corner of the sheet in her left hand.

"Pardon me," she said, and whipped off the cotton covering. He opened his eyes, and saw her, and spurted like a whale.

It was a very rude awakening.

He stared at the hooded figure by his bed. The horror in those eyes, the slowly dawning horror in those eyes, was something she would hug to her heart through many a long night. For the first time in her life, she looked into a man's face and saw fear flickering back at her.

"Alone at last," she said. "The three of us."

Imagine, just imagine, waking up to see her by your bed. The woman of your dirty dreams is standing by your bed. The woman of your slimy thoughts, the woman of your dark desires, is standing – with a hammer – by your bed.

She's taking off her crimson scarf and grinning as she watches you. You haven't seen her grin before. You've barely seen her smile.

She's grinning like the peasant grins, before he forks the landlord. A prison-burning sort of grin. A worm-is-turning sort of grin. And Timothy, poor Timothy, has woken up to that.

57

She struck him with the hammer on his cheek. A casual, glancing blow that was not too hard. Just enough to crack the bone. She hammered him again, to impress upon him that he was no longer dreaming. She hammered him again, to keep up the momentum. And she hammered him again, for the hell of it.

Even Bella, even brittle little Bella, can lift a hammer. Even she can hold it in her hands, and swing it high, and bring it down. The crunch of metal on bone was a fairly unusual sound. Had she played cricket, it might have suggested leather on willow. But she hadn't, so it didn't.

The foundations of his world were being shaken so fiercely that he hardly remembered to scream, and for one ghastly moment she thought he might be going into a state of catatonic shock, which would have denied her the human interaction she valued so highly.

But then he put a hand to his face, and touched the wetness. He held the hand in front of him, and looked at the strawberry stain dripping from his fingers. His mouth sagged open and some strange sound came out, some grunt of disbelief that she couldn't quite catch, and which was therefore lost to posterity. His face crumpled, and he began to blub. He howled like a baby. She smiled fondly at him and gazed down at the delicate and rapidly shrivelling flower that nestled shyly between his thighs.

She felt an overwhelming and inexplicable desire to talk to him, to fill in the gaps, to humanise the one she was about to pulverise.

"Well," she said, brightly. "This is jolly, isn't it?"

Small-talk was not her strength.

She struck him again, breaking his nose. Blood gushed out. His tears turned the blood almost pink as it ran into the open mouth. He was sitting up in bed. Sitting in his own slime. And he didn't know whether to protect his head or his nose or his groin. (Not that she would have pummelled his trembling privates. She's not the type to hit a man below the belt.)

Things were not going well for Timothy. Timothy was in a state of profound confusion. And Bella, because she is someone who *empathises*, because she is a sentient creature with nerve-ends that quiver at the slightest touch, understood the cosmic terror that must be clutching him.

She understood the fear that must be turning his bowels to butter. She understood the vomit-panic that must be churning through him. She understood because she'd been there, she'd followed that route, she'd travelled down that tunnel and come out the other side.

But what she couldn't understand, what she couldn't quite comprehend, was why he hadn't tried to grab the hammer from her hand. What she couldn't quite cope with was why he was just sitting there, emasculated, in a little pool of his own mess.

He said nothing. It was strange the way he sobbed and bled and said nothing. Strange and yet familiar. As if he couldn't change it, so had to endure it.

Bella wondered for a moment what train of events had brought Timothy to such a sorry pass. Maybe his mother told him what a good-looking boy he was, as she filled him with egg fingers. Maybe she told him no woman would be good enough for her boy, and maybe he believed it.

Or maybe she was the other sort of mother. The mother who has motherhood thrust upon her. Maybe she had a stomach cramp, and went to the ladies', and Bob's your uncle, fancy that, out he popped. Pink and wrinkled and oozing from every orifice.

And maybe it just wasn't her thing, the milkiness of it all. Maybe she locked him in the coal shed, or spanked him with a Brillo pad, or discussed his smalls with the neighbours, or interfered with him on his sixteenth birthday.

Whichever way you look at it, Mummy is to blame.

Poor little Timmy-boy. Poor little Tim-Tims. It's not his fault at all. It's really not his fault at all. You can see poor little Timmies on the telly all the time. The inmates of special units. The lifers who've destroyed lives.

You see them on the screen, trying not to smirk as they sit there in their freshly laundered linen. They come out with all the jargon. They tell you in that Grendon whine about the therapy they've had, how they've talked it through, how they've come to terms with what they did. And running through it all, bubbling away beneath the surface, you hear the self-justifying snivel of the unrepentant rapist.

They think, by doing time, they've done their penance to society. Except they didn't victimise society. Not all of it. Not the bit that matters. They didn't do their damage to society. They haven't made society too scared to walk the streets. It's not society they've scarred.

If you hear them say they're sorry, don't believe it. They're never sorry, and it wouldn't make a difference if they were. But if they say it, if they ever dare to say it, don't believe it. They're lying scum for whom castration is the kindest cut of all.

So it's time to despatch Timmy. Time to send Timbo to that sluice-hole in the sky. She gripped the hammer in both hands and held it high above her head.

"Prepare to meet your Maker, but first the Undertaker."

And with that brief eulogy, those few apt words, that short rhyme which the ever-creative, ever-poetic Bella almost coined there and then, she brought the hammer down, she swung it down, she slammed it down with all her might.

The blow struck him on top of his head, and his body jerked up, and a soft groan parted his lips. Watery liquid splashed her hands. Dark spots spattered the wall, spreading like ink on blotting paper.

She struck him again, and it was like cracking an egg, like hitting the shell with a spoon, like having an early breakfast in Brighton. She pulled the claw out of his skull, and chewed her lip, and pounded him. She hammered her message home the only way she could. She bludgeoned him for all her silent sisters. She battered the bones that protected his brain, and she almost cried as he almost died.

60

Her hand held the hammer and the hammer swung down. She pulped his head. She smashed it. She mashed the morsels that lay inside. She heard a last and muted moan. He stopped twitching and lay still. Timothy's life ended with both a bang and a whimper. With her final blow, she terminated that particular cycle of deprivation forever.

There are certain laws of nature, she reflected, certain iron laws, that you flout at your peril. People in glass houses shouldn't throw stones. Men with thin skulls shouldn't try to involve randomly selected women in their fantasies.

She looked at him. She looked at the mess she'd made of him, and the mess he'd made in his bed. Had his soul not already fled his inert body, he would surely have recoiled at the sludge of substances in which he lay. His sheets were soiled with nocturnal secretions, the cream laced with red like a raspberry ripple.

She put her fingers on his skin. It felt warm to the touch. He looked surprised, if not amazed. He must have been mid-twenties. She couldn't tell. They say the best die young, which goes to show how much they know. He broke her hammer, in the end. The head flew off. It might have hurt her, if she hadn't seen it coming.

She slumped down on the edge of the bed. She felt limp from it all. It's not easy, what she did. She tried to catch her breath from the sudden and unpractised exertion, moving his left knee so it didn't dig in. She was tired and weak and hungry. He'd exhausted her, as she knew he would.

She leaned over and placed the hammer on his bedside table. His bed felt soft. She didn't know how people could sleep on such soft beds. The bed was like a hammock. He lay in the scoop of his hammock, eyeing the wardrobe. She wished she could have watched him begin to decompose. She wished she could have waited as he flaked away. He oozed in his hammock. She shook her head regretfully. She should have asked him how he got her number.

His wardrobe was crammed with clothes. It was jammed

61

with jackets. She ran her fingers through his pockets, and placed her findings on the floor. A little heap of his personal effects grew like a wart on the carpet. Cash, bits of plastic, keys. A calf-skin wallet. She flicked it open. It was stuffed with notes. She couldn't help noticing the notes. Wads of tempting twenties. She took it all. It was the spoils of war, and she took it all.

She liked his kitchen. It was nicer than her kitchen. Her kitchen was lit by neon light, the sort of harsh strip-light that strips you bare. His kitchen was a warm kitchen. Cosy was the word she would have used, had she wanted to describe it. She took brown bread from the bread-basket. The fridge was full, which showed he planned ahead.

She left the cooked half-chicken. Too many bacteria in cold meats. She slit open a packet of fresh cheddar. It was mature cheddar, which was her second favourite. She hoped it wouldn't give her nightmares. She shredded the iceberg lettuce and sliced two green tomatoes. She put the bread and cheese and salad on one of the dinner plates and sat at the kitchen table.

She ate slowly and methodically. Her hand was smarting as she lifted bread to her mouth. The skin of her palm was scraped. It looked like a rope burn. The thin velvet of her velvet gloves hadn't helped. There was nothing to read while she ate, and no-one to talk to. A solitary meal.

She filled the kettle, and dropped a teabag into a beige mug, and spooned in three spoons of sugar. Waste not, want not, and she needed the energy. She poured out boiling water and pressed the teabag with the spoon until the water turned brown. She added a drop of milk and stirred.

Timothy had once been, and was no more. Timothy was now a has-been. She held the mug up, as if in salute, and smiled at the cooker. Absent friends, and she toasted his recent and involuntary demise.

She made him disappear. She disappeared him. She came into his home and hammered him. She stood beside his bed and watched him bleed. She sipped the tea and thought of him. His splayed and splintered form, the milky gore he gushed.

It frightened her to think of him. She felt nothing when she thought of him, and it frightened her.

# CHAPTER EIGHT

She slept the sleep of the just, and woke up thinking guns, the way one does.

She was thinking how they shone, when they caught the light. The dull metal shine of the well-polished weapon. The glinting smoking glory of an automatic gun. The power that comes bursting from its barrel. The mustn't-nibble forbidden fruit of a civilised society. The heavy metal feeling when you hold it in your hand.

She was thinking how badly she needed a gun. Any gun. A musket gun. A rifle gun. A carbine gun. A gimme-the-money-and-run gun. A catch-me-if-you-can gun.

She was thinking explosives. She was thinking sawn-offs. Flame-throwers, cannon and cordite. Dynamite, gelignite, sheer delight. She was thinking tactics. She was thinking strategy.

Bella's thoughts, as can be seen, were tinged with a certain martial vigour. She was tending to the militant. Bella was thinking ballistics, when she woke up. She was thinking Brownings, Brens and bazookas, as she stretched and yawned in her bed. Bella was thinking remarkably big.

It was past noon when she woke. It was past lunchtime on a Brighton Saturday. A Brighton Saturday is unlike any other Saturday. Maybe it's the sea air. Maybe it's the salt in the sea air that goes to your head.

Whatever it is, you know when the weekend hits Brighton. All chains are slightly loosened on Saturday. The chains that bind you tight all week are slightly loosened on Saturday.

Even Bella's chains, which were already looser than most, would loosen further that Saturday.

There are several gunshops in Sussex. Some of them also sell fishing tackle. They are fishermen's friends, as if gun-freaks and angling-freaks were flesh of one flesh. They sell thigh-high rubber waders and hooks and lines and country clothing.

But the one she chose was a pure gunshop, a chaste gunshop, a gunshop that held fast to its faith. It was a fundamentalist gunshop, not an ecumenical gunshop. It pandered to no-one, and it promised nothing. What you saw was what you got, and what you got was what you wanted.

She entered, unannounced, and stared in awe and wonder. Target pistols and hunting knives and single-action airguns and double-barrelled shotguns. An emporium of armament.

Bella was in paradise.

Rifles fixed to the wall like icons. Pistols on velvet cushions beneath glass counters. The smells of gun-oil and grease and tobacco and sweat. The punters with their survival magazines, sucked in off the street by fear and loathing.

Soft-spoken men whose hatred thickened the air. So many tattoos in blues and blacks on so many patches of pure white skin. Such hooded eyes, such padded jackets, such brooding stares, such paranoia prodding them from behind. She'd come for protection against the crazies, but the crazies had got there first.

A man in an anorak was watching her. They were all

65

watching her, but he watched her more closely, more brazenly, and with more interest, than the others. He was holding something wrapped in canvas under his arm. He looked like the sort of man who used to enter her nightmares.

"You been here before?"

His hair was cropped close to the scalp. He smelt of dog. She shook her head. She'd never been there before. She was a virgin in the world of weapons.

"I think I've seen you here before."

His skin was stretched taut over high cheekbones. Pale eyes flicked across her face, searching for alien features. He stood stiffly, as if afraid of being ambushed.

"Must be someone else," she said.

They were the first words she'd spoken since she'd said her goodbyes to Timothy. She wondered if he could hear it in her voice. It was the afternoon after the night before, and she wondered if it showed.

"You must be thinking of someone else."

"I'm sure it was you."

"I think not," she said. "Sorry."

Old habits die hard. Bella was reared to be polite. She was educated to be sensitive. She was raised to say no with a self-deprecating smile and a regretful tilt of the head. Whatever you lose, you never lose your manners.

"All the same . . . " he said.

"Afraid not."

She was surprised to see how hurt he looked, in a belligerent sort of way. She is basically a kind person, and she didn't want to hurt him. She didn't want to squash him. She didn't want him to think her – heaven forfend – a snob. So it seemed only polite to maintain the dialogue.

"Were you in the Forces?"

"Could've been," he said. "Could've if I wanted to."

He didn't blink often. He might miss something.

"You looking or buying, then?"

"Just browsing."

"I'm buying," he said. "You've got to, these days."

Got to? Surely only Bella has got to buy. Surely she alone is impelled to part with her hard-earned in exchange for the only phallus worth having, the smoothest, sleekest and most user-friendly phallus there was.

"Why have you got to buy, liebchen? Have I missed something?"

He gave her a pitying look.

"Why you've got to buy," he said, "is to be prepared. If you don't stick up for your own, no-one else will. We've got to stick together. Know what I mean?"

She nodded. She knew what he meant. She always knew what everyone meant.

"They'll take over if we don't stick together. I'm a kith and kin man. They've got theirs and we've got ours. No mixing. I don't believe in mixing."

She smiled at him. It was her special smile. Her please go away you piece of sub-proletarian turd smile. A subtle smile, whose subtleties escaped him.

"Separate but equal, as they say."

He tapped the side of his forehead.

"Only natural, anyway. We've got the brains."

He lowered his voice.

"They come running down my road, and they'll be sorry. I won't mess about when they come running down my road."

"I'm sure you won't."

"Damn right I won't."

And then he stopped and gazed at her and pressed his loose lips tightly together. Grimly, wearily, commando-style, as if he were just back from a bad tour of the Falls. Daring her to disagree.

"Well," she said, finally, to break the silence. "Well, that's very interesting."

"Stan."

"That's very interesting, Stan," she said. "Really very interesting. Very interesting indeed."

67

When certain people talk to you, you shouldn't say anything encouraging back. You really shouldn't say anything at all. Stan was one of those people.

Stan often spoke to women. He spoke to women at bus-stops and in waiting-rooms and in lifts. He especially liked speaking to women in lifts, if there were just the two of them. He'd press the stop button and the lift would stick between floors. He'd had some of his best conversations in lifts.

Women liked talking to Stan. He knew that for a fact, because they told him so. When he let the doors slide back, he always asked whether they'd enjoyed the conversation, and they always said they had. Stan didn't think he'd ever met a woman who hadn't enjoyed talking to him.

He took out a handkerchief and coughed into it, then held it slightly away from him. Bella stared at the glob of yellow sputum at its centre. That's also interesting, Stan, she wanted to say. So many things she wants to say, that she must leave unsaid.

He began again. "Can't be very nice being a woman . . . "

"It has its problems."

" . . . not a decent woman . . . "

"You're so right, Stan."

" . . . not with them moving in everywhere . . . "

"Stan, this is Sussex."

" . . . can't feel safe in your own bed . . . "

"I really don't see . . . "

He peered at her suspiciously.

"Of course," he said, "some women prefer them. So I've heard. Go sniffing round their clubs like bitches on heat."

He came closer and hissed out the words.

"They're not bigger, you know. That's a myth."

"If you say so."

"I do say so."

And he jabbed an angry forefinger within an inch of her face.

68

A heavenly vision floated into her head: Stan mashed, Stan smashed, Stan pulped on his pillow. Stan battered, Stan bludgeoned, Stan bleeding. Stan, Stan, the mincemeat man.

She'd scrape out the toilet-wall philosophy. She'd give him a migraine he wouldn't forget. She'd crack open his cranium. She'd lobotomise him. She'd give his brain a D and C, she'd . . .

"Why are you smiling?"

"What?"

"I said why are you smiling?"

"Am I smiling?"

"You've got a smile on your face, so you're smiling."

"I must be thinking happy thoughts."

"It's rude to smile."

"I'm never rude."

"You think I'm funny?"

"I think you're tragic."

"What does that mean?"

"It means I don't think you're funny."

He gave her a look. He had a vague sense that she might be laughing at him. That smile on her face. That smirk. Like she knew something he didn't. But no-one ever laughed at Stan. They just had to look at him, and they knew not to laugh. They knew what he'd do if they did.

He realised, with relief, that she must be dim. She was smiling because she was a dimwit. Slow on the uptake. Out to lunch. Feeble-minded. Generally womanish.

He shifted his weight to the other leg.

"I think you need a helping hand," he said. "I think you don't know what to do. You're bewildered. That's why you're grinning like that. Because you're bewildered. You tell me what your problem is, you tell Stan, and I'll tell you what to do."

She could have told him. She could have told Stan her problem. Had she been alone with him, she probably would have told Stan her problem. But not here. Not without a weapon. She left the bold words unsaid, she swallowed down her bile, and wiped off the sneer that so enraged them all.

For Bella was still in her bourgeois phase. Bella was still held back by etiquette, and innate breeding, and the thought of his boot in her belly.

"You're very clever aren't you, Stan?"

"I wouldn't say I'm *very* clever . . . "

"I mean you've got a lot of knowledge."

"I know a thing or two."

"You know a thing or two about guns."

"I know everything about guns."

"Tell me what type of gun to get."

"What do you want it for?"

"I want to shoot it."

"What at?"

"Difficult to say," she said.

"There's clay-pigeons, paper targets, plinking in the yard. You tell me what you'll be shooting at, and I'll tell you what gun to get."

She thought. She pondered. She weighed up. How best to put it?

"I live in a basement, Stan. It's not a very nice basement. It's a fairly dark basement, and a fairly damp basement. I get fairly depressed in my basement, Stan."

"I'm sorry to hear it."

"And to top it all, to cap it all, to crown it all, I've got another problem."

She paused. He waited.

"I've got what's known as a vermin problem."

"Rodents and suchlike?"

She smiled. "Suchlike."

Stan looked concerned.

"You need a shotgun. That's what you need. I've got a couple myself. You can't go wrong with a shotgun, is what I always say."

He scratched his shaven head.

70

"Bit dodgy for a flat, though. Flats and shotguns," he sucked air through his teeth, "that's a bit dodgy."

"What's your advice, then?"

"Get an air-rifle, is my advice."

He was thinking hard.

"Or poison."

"Poison?"

"Cyanide. Paraquat. You name it."

"I don't think I could," she said.

"Why not?"

"I wouldn't want them to suffer . . . " she searched for the right word, " . . . unnecessarily."

Bella the moralist. Bella the suddenly squeamish. Bella the big-hearted hangwoman.

"They're only rats, for God's sake."

"I know they are, but all the same . . . "

He shook his head.

"You women are too soft."

"Yet supple."

"That's why you get walked on."

"Because we're soft?"

"Because you're women."

"Do you like women, Stan?"

"They're all right."

He glanced at her warily. She might be after his body, or even his shotgun.

"Look," he said. "Look . . . "

"Yes, Stan?"

"I've got to go now."

She nodded.

"I've got to feed Paisley."

"Alsatian?"

"Pit bull." He shifted the canvas package to the other arm. "Do you like dogs?"

Bella reflects. To her all dogs are male, the way all cats are female. Dogs hunt in packs and stink out the house and grovel before their mistresses. They are the natural fascists of the animal world. Stroke them and they bite your hand. Beat them and they love you forever.

"They do have a certain appeal," she said. "A canine servility that can be balm to the soul."

He gave her a hard look. He gave her one of the hardest of his hard looks.

"Well," he said. "That's all right, then."

He backed towards the door, groping in his pocket for the great simplicities he'd come in with.

"It's been a very pleasant conversation, all the same," he said.

And he exited sideways, like a crab. The door banged shut behind Stan the Man. Universal suffrage, she realised, had been a great mistake.

"You looking for anything special, love?"

She turned towards the new voice. One of the assistants was speaking to her as he dismantled a full-bore. The grease-tin was open and ready. She approached the counter.

"She wants a Saturday-night-special," someone called out.

Soft laughter surged to the ceiling. The Saturday-night-special. The Yankee woman's friend. The palmable, pocketable, affordable little weapon that will see you through the night.

Amerika. Land of opportunity and self-expression and serial murders. You go there and first you lose yourself and then you find yourself. Glory, glory, glory. The endless possibilities of the endless freeways ribboning across the desert.

"Tell me what you want, love."

What Bella wants. What Bella wants is what she can't have. What she wants is open windows on summer nights. Lone walks along the shore. No fear of the motorway breakdown. No terror of the dark. No horror of the gang. No comments in the street. No furtive touchings on the Tube. No more stroking their egos for fear of the fist in the face,

72

the broken nose, the blood and snot running into her mouth. Bella was born free and is everywhere in chains. Usurpers have stolen her inheritance, and she must reclaim it.

"It's not fair," she said.

"I know it's not."

"I want them to leave me alone. That's all."

"Home protection," he said. "That's what we call it in the trade."

He put a small brown box on the counter and removed the lid.

"These are going like hot cakes. Can't get enough of them."

He took out a snub-nosed gun with a wooden handle. She reached across and ran a finger lightly along the barrel.

"It's an air revolver," he said. "You've got five shots at any intruder. Target pistols are no good, because you've got to reload after each pellet. With this you can relax. If you miss the first time – and you'll always miss the first time – you'll get him the second time or the third."

"What if he's moving as I fire?"

"Ask him to stand still." He held the gun in his palm. "They're very popular with taxi drivers. And women living alone. Single mothers, and suchlike. Your only problem is whether to go for a four-inch barrel or a two-inch. This one's a two-inch. Neat and unobtrusive. Nice balance."

He opened the chamber and spun it with his thumb.

"Ladies like it," he said. "Why don't you have a go?"

He picked up a red tin of pellets and walked her across to the indoor range in the opposite corner. He unscrewed the golden shells.

"Remove the cone, pop in the pellet, screw it back on, into the chamber, and you're away." He loaded up and snapped the chamber shut and put the gun on the counter. "Try it."

She picked it up. Heavier than she'd imagined. Smooth and chunky. Short barrel glinting dully. She held it with both hands, closed one eye and sighted on the target.

A journey of a thousand miles begins with but a single step. Steady, Bella, steady. Make my day, punk. Just evening up the odds, a little. There are murderers, victims and bystanders, and they won't let me be a bystander. Better the butcher than the lamb. Nothing's ordained. Whatever I wear, wherever I go. Welcome to my death-wish. Steady, hold it steady . . .

Let them quake when we walk behind them. Let them quicken their steps, and hunch their shoulders, and hurry home in the dusk. Scurry home, dogs. Avert your eyes as we pass. Let fear creep up and whisper in your ear . . .

Swill-fed pigs. Snivelling toads. Syphilitic scum. Nothing you were, and nothing you shall be. The dust in my eye. The shit on my shoes . . .

She held her breath and squeezed the trigger. Light pressure, don't jerk it. Be gentle, gentle Bella. The hammer hit the shell. Compressed air sent the pellet flying towards the target. The shock of the bang and the gun lifting in her hand.

"That's good. Now relax and fire the rest. There's four more. That's good. You're doing good."

She pulled back the hammer. The chamber revolved. She squeezed the trigger. The crack of the shot reverberated inside her skull. She pulled the trigger until the bangs stopped coming. She could have pulled that trigger forever. She could have kept on squeezing and kept on shooting. She could have heard those bangs forever.

A whirring noise and the paper target was pulleyed up to them. He unclipped it and counted the holes.

"Four out of five. Your first one missed because you were tense. You've got good hits. Two on the inner circle and two on the bull."

He grinned at her, pleased with his pupil.

"You'll be okay. Someone comes in your window, just aim at his face and let him have five."

They went back to the counter. He removed the shells from the chamber and began to press the rubber seals back into the cones.

"Are you taking it, then?" he asked, without looking up. "How much?"

"A hundred and twenty for cash. And I'll pump up the shells for you."

Pump up the shells?

"Pump up the *shells*?"

"It comes with a hand-pump. You have to pump up the shell again before you put a fresh pellet in."

"What about the bullets?"

He slowly raised his head.

"There aren't any bullets."

He tapped the red tin.

"It fires pellets. It uses air to fire pellets. That's why it's called an airgun."

"But I want to fire bullets, not pellets!"

He looked at her. He sighed. He shook his head. He put the gun back in its box like a jeweller who discovers the customer can't afford the price.

"We can't sell that sort of thing over the counter. They're not sweets, you know. They're dangerous. You might accidentally kill someone."

This to Bella, who has never killed anyone accidentally in her life. The vision of the gun began to fade, like a guttering candle.

"And you need a licence," he added, snapping a rubber band around the box and replacing the box beneath the counter. A man in a cashmere coat was standing nearby.

"We can't sell them to just anyone. If we could sell them to just anyone, Stan could have one." The argument had an iron logic.

"Who gives out the licence?"

"The police," the assistant said, with quiet satisfaction. "First you register with the police, then they check you out, and if you've been a good girl, and if you've got no form, and if they think your reasons are valid," and he stressed the last word, "you get your licence."

"And if not, you don't," the cashmere coat added.

The assistant shrugged.

"There you are," he said. "You don't want to go shooting live ammunition anyway."

"No," she agreed.

She smiled her thanks.

Gimme the gun, you bum.

"I don't suppose I do."

# CHAPTER NINE

She stood outside the shop with light flakes of snow falling on her bare head. Deflated. The momentum suddenly halted. The adrenalin gradually leaking away. She began walking down the road, going nowhere.

Damn them. Damn them all. Damn all the legislators with their well-protected privacy. Damn them to hell and back, and damn their lousy gun-licences.

Damn them for leaving her defenceless. Damn them for saying she couldn't keep a gun in her bag, or a knife or a CS spray. Damn them for the curfew they kept her under, for the purdah they placed her in, for the invisible chador they wrapped around her so that her form wouldn't offend. Damn all the legislating dogs, and damn their judges, and damn the strength that kept them safe.

Bella walking down the road, spitting silent curses into the falling snow. Bella thwarted, on the brink. Bloody Bella. Bloody, bold and resolute. Vengeance beckoning like a beacon on the horizon, and she couldn't reach it.

Bella trudging down the road. Cold and wet and weaponless. It's funny, really. You think it's funny? Don't laugh too loud. Don't laugh too loud or she'll hear you. Ask not for whom the Bella tolls. She just might toll for you.

Footsteps behind her. She tensed. They came nearer. She

didn't turn. Footsteps beside her and she waited for them to pass, but they slowed and fell into step. She stared straight ahead and kept on walking.

"Do you want to mug me, untermensch?"

"I couldn't help overhearing . . . "

She stole a sideways look at her fellow-traveller. It was the man in the cashmere coat. She carried on down the road.

"I couldn't help hearing what you said in there," he continued. "You did it all wrong, you know."

He had a long, loping stride which he was trying, with difficulty, to shorten.

"People who want shooters don't go barging into gun-shops."

It hadn't occurred to her that what she wanted was a shooter. Shooters were what gangsters used. Shooters were used by villains and rogues and ne'er-do-wells. Mobsters and racketeers. Nasty, brutish people who didn't pay their taxes.

But when you really think of it, what's in a word? The law-makers have their legal guns. The law-breakers have their shooters. They've built their barricade, and they've shoved her over the other side, and no semantic quibble can stop her now.

"Where do they go then?"

"They come to me."

And he peeled off towards a white estate parked across the road. He put the key in the lock and glanced back at her.

"Coming?"

She shivered in the cold. She watched him get into the car. She watched the maybe gun-dealer slide into the car. May be a gun-dealer, and may be not. That is indeed the question. Is he just after her money? Are his intentions therefore honourable? She watched him settle in the driver's seat.

It's a funny way to find customers. But business is

business, after all. He might be for real. But he might be a fake. She watched him clip on the belt. This is her moment of decision. She'll decide how much she needs a gun. How much she aches for a gun. How much she'll gamble, to get her gun.

She crossed the slushy road and walked round to the passenger door. He leaned across and pushed it open. She stared at him, and for a moment she hesitated.

She tried to read his face, but his face gave nothing away. He was a big man, and he had big hands. Big, square, farmworker's hands. She pictured those hands around her neck. The unhurried squeezing of his big, square hands.

She knows her fragility excites them. She knows her weakness makes them want her. They only have to look at her, and they hear the sound of bones snapping. They only have to breathe on her, and she bruises.

So she hesitated, for a moment. She saw his hands and she hesitated. She saw his face and she hesitated. But only for a moment, for she who hesitates is lost. She who hesitates will never buy a chic little matt-black shooter from a man in a cashmere coat.

She slipped into the passenger seat, and closed the door. He pumped the throttle. The car surged forward down the empty road.

# CHAPTER TEN

"I didn't quite catch your name," she said, watching his hands on the wheel. Every few seconds his eyes flicked up to the rearview mirror.

"Mr Brown." He accelerated through an amber light.

"And you are . . . ?"

"Miss Jones."

"Pleased to meet you, Miss Jones."

"And you, Mr Brown."

He drove hard and fast. A man in a hurry. He kept his foot on the pedal and powered down the road. The speed pushed her back in her seat, like when a plane takes off. She likes that feeling. She likes the feeling you get when the plane takes off and you're forced back in your seat.

She's never had much sense of direction. She's always been fairly directionless. After fifteen minutes or so, she had lost her bearings completely. When he took a left, and then a right, and then another left, and pulled off on to a piece of waste ground, he did it so quickly that by the time he'd braked to a halt and doused the lights she was still fumbling to undo the seatbelt.

He pointed to a small switch on the dashboard.

"You know what that does, Miss Jones?"

He pressed it down.

"It locks all the doors. This is a car with central locking, Miss Jones."

Taste the infinite vulnerability of Bella. To get the gun, she must enter a stranger's car. To enter a stranger's car is to risk all. To risk all can be to lose all.

They sat in their seats in the gathering dusk. He tapped the top of the gearstick with a thick, gloved finger. She watched the finger move up and down, like a baton marking time. Such huge hands, he has.

"Are you the law, Miss Jones?"

"I'm sorry?"

He turned in his seat and gripped her shoulder.

"Are you a plod of the female persuasion?"

He switched on the vanity light so they could see each other's eyes. He had blank, impassive, colourless eyes. She'd never seen such colourless eyes. She didn't know they made such colourless eyes. She wondered who had drained the colour from his colourless eyes.

"No," she said. "I'm not."

"That's a double negative, Miss Jones."

"But true all the same."

His lips pulled back over strong yellow teeth. Her stomach began to churn.

"You might be wired up," he said. "You might, at this moment, be transmitting to some pals in an unmarked transit. And that would be very naughty, Miss Jones, very naughty indeed."

His fingers dug into her thin shoulder.

"You've got a suspicious mind, Mr Brown. I want to buy a gun. You want to sell me a gun. We're made for each other."

"I fear not, Miss Jones. Women are not one of my weaknesses. The female form is not to my taste."

"How so?"

"The curves get on my nerves."

"You mean I'm doing business with a bumboy, Mr Brown?"

He looked aggrieved.

81

"I am not a poofter, Miss Jones. I am a dominant male. Please pass me your handbag."

She handed it across. He took off the gloves. He opened the bag and emptied its contents into his lap. He ran his fingers over the lining, then spent some minutes examining the assorted items he'd removed, before dropping them back in and clicking the bag shut.

"That's fine, Miss Jones."

He placed the bag on top of the dashboard.

"Please put your hands on your head."

She rolled her eyes in a show of boredom, a little display of protest, a small token of resistance. But he was very big. And she was very small. So she did as she was told and put her hands on her head.

He frisked her very fast and very thoroughly, using a light, firm pressure as he felt all the places you would expect a microphone to be taped, and some you would not.

When he finished he put his gloves back on and passed the handbag back to her and switched on the ignition.

"Please accept my apologies," he said. "I can assure you that was even more distasteful for me than it must have been for you."

He edged back on to the highway and drove along for about ten minutes before taking the Newhaven road. They sped over the Downs and up to the coast, then turned west towards Brighton. Near Rottingdean he pulled into a pub forecourt. She looked at the thatched roof and half-timbered frontage. It was an Olde Englande kind of pub. Tudor or Elizabethan. Something like that. She doesn't know much about architecture, but she knows, as they say, what she likes.

"I'm dropping you here," he said. "Wait for me inside."

"How long will you be?"

"Not long."

"How long's not long?"

"Don't rush me, Miss Jones."

She undid the seatbelt and clutched her handbag and glared at him.

"You don't even know exactly what I want."

"Do you know what you want?"

She considered for a moment.

"I want a handgun," she said. "In good order. Oiled and ready and preferably automatic."

"How much ammunition?"

"Heaps of it. Piles of the stuff. Mountains of it. I want to jingle with it as I walk. I want to be weighed down with it. I need a year's supply. I need a year's supply, at the very least. If not more."

"I can get you one clip."

"How many bullets in a clip?"

"Six."

"As in six hundred?"

"As in six."

"How can six bullets last me a whole year?"

"You fire one every two months."

"Fair enough."

"It'll cost you four hundred."

"A bit steep."

"It's a seller's market."

He flicked off the central locking. She stepped out of the car. He circled round and wound down his window.

"You've got the cash on you?"

"Of course."

"Where did you hide it?"

Warm light glowed behind the leaded windows. She was in dire need of a drink.

"Nowhere you'd want to look, Mr Brown."

And she smiled at him, and he smiled at her, and she watched the two red tail-lights surge away and disappear down the road.

She entered the pub. She crossed the threshold, passed by the cloakrooms, and into the lounge bar. It was a very

Rottingdean sort of pub. Salubrious would be the word. It had the kind of shabby plushness that the better sort of Saxon prefers. There were no foaming slops on the floor. There was no juke-box in the corner. No yobbery spitting in each other's beer. A very clean, very Rottingdean, sort of pub.

A few solitary drinkers sat at separate tables so they wouldn't have to talk to anyone. A young couple nursed their glasses in a corner, touching and whispering and laughing. She went into the ladies' and closed the cubicle door behind her.

Good old Tim-Tims, she thought. She removed a thick roll of moist notes from her most precious place. Good old Timbo. She peeled off the polythene they'd been wrapped in and counted out four hundred. She put the remaining three hundred and twenty into the zip compartment of her bag and pulled the chain. The previous day's *Guardian* was propped up by the sink. It was a very nice pub.

Back in the bar, she sat down as near to the fire as she could and lit a cigarette. She toyed with the idea of ordering a drink, but decided to wait. She would wait until her gun-dealer returned. She would let him ply her with drink. She would let him stick his hand in his pocket and pull out a wad and ask her what she wanted. What'll it be, he'd say. What's your pleasure, he'd ask.

Bella's pleasure. Bella's pleasure is to let them buy her drinks. Bella's pleasure is to watch the three-legs spend their money. Bella's pleasure is to make them fork out a fiver or two. She can't help it. She likes it when they buy her things. To make them pay is a woman's way. A small and tacky victory perhaps, but it tastes so sweet.

He came in twenty minutes later, with his cashmere coat over his arm and a tight little smile on his face. He draped the coat carefully over a chair and straightened up and ran a hand over his hair. They nodded with cautious intimacy at each other.

"Would you care for a drink, Miss Jones?"

"A Babycham would be nice, Mr Brown."

Little miss innocent. Little miss Babycham. Little miss butter wouldn't melt. She blew smoke up at the ceiling and watched it curl slowly around dark wooden rafters. She was beginning to feel slightly tired and slightly edgy. There was so much to do, and so little time in which to do it.

She watched him as he walked up to the bar. He spoke quietly to the barman and handed over a large-looking note. The barman gave a murmured reply and they both laughed. Male bonding, she reflected, is a wonderful thing. He came back and put her drink on the small square mat and sat down. He drew his chair up to the table, and suddenly she couldn't wait any longer.

"Let's do the deal."

"Patience is a virtue, Miss Jones."

"Not one of mine, Mr Brown. Not any more."

"All in good time, Miss Jones."

He held up a full glass. Golden liquid swirled inside.

"All things come to she who waits."

Steel-grey hair covered his skull in wispy strands. She could see the shape of his skull very clearly. She had become very conscious of the shape of men's skulls.

She puffed on her cigarette, and saw him scowl. She groaned inwardly. Another non-smoker. No lectures, please. Not today. Not now.

"Filthy habit, Miss Jones, if you don't mind my saying so."

She smiled at him and sucked smoke deep into her lungs.

"You don't indulge then, Mr Brown?"

He swallowed Scotch and grimaced.

"Never seen the need to, myself. Healthy mind in a healthy body, and that's how I intend to keep it."

"You look pretty fit," she remarked.

"I am pretty fit."

"You go jogging, I suppose."

He pulled a face.

"Jogging's a joke. I do proper exercises. Forty minutes each day. Bend and stretch. Press-ups. Jerk-ups. Lift-ups. Marvellous feeling. Work up a healthy sweat. Can't beat it."

Well bully for you, baby. Bully for you.

"They say smokers want to go back to the teat," he said. "So they say."

She took a last drag and exhaled slowly and thoughtfully.

"Is that a fact, Mr Brown?"

"They say smokers are oral people," he continued. Tiny blue veins patterned his cheeks. "Are you an oral person, Miss Jones?"

"Apparently."

She ground the stub into the ashtray.

"Whereas you're obviously anal." Like the police, she prefers to get her retaliation in first.

His flint eyes narrowed for a moment but he kept the smile. She was the customer, after all.

"With a mouth like yours, Miss Jones, you need a gun."

She took another cigarette from the pack and put it between her lips. He picked up her lighter and flicked it on. He held the flame to the end of the weed. She watched the tip glow red. She could have told him, if he'd asked, that smoking wouldn't kill her. Whatever put her in her grave, it wouldn't be tobacco.

"How did you get into this game, Mr Brown?"

"What game?"

"The dealing game. The wheeling and dealing game."

"That's a teeny bit personal, Miss Jones. Just a weeny bit."

"Didn't mean to pry . . . " she said.

"I'm sure you didn't."

" . . . but I'd be interested to know."

He downed more Scotch.

"It's like anything else. You find your source. You find your market. You put the two together and you give them what they need."

"Just like that?"

"Just like that."

"Do you sell to anyone?"

"Anyone who's got the money."

"What if you don't like their politics?"

"I don't like most people's politics, Miss Jones. I probably wouldn't like yours."

"You a true-blue, Mr Brown?"

"Through and through. Self-made and proud of it."

"You don't like unions, then."

"I detest unions. Troublemakers, Miss Jones. Saboteurs. The enemy within."

"What about the little man?"

"Sod the little man."

"Were you born like that, Mr Brown, or were you made?"

"A bit of both, Miss Jones. I joined up. I signed on. I took the Queen's shilling and I did my bit. Twelve years, my love. Twelve good years. The army made me. I went in a know-nothing. A simpleton who thought he was a smart-arse. And I came out a staff sergeant."

He took another swig.

"Military Police, Miss Jones. A redcap."

He smiled as he remembered.

"You didn't see action, then?"

He gazed at her with his colourless eyes.

"Course I saw action."

He had a deadpan way of speaking. Like nothing really bothered him. Like he'd been chilled to the core and he couldn't get warm again. Like he was ready to chop down every law to build his fire.

"Straightening out the scumbags they sent us was action. Beating shit out of malingering dossers was action. I did my bit, Miss Jones, don't you worry."

"Sounds as if you liked it, Mr Brown."

"I loved it, Miss Jones."

"Sorry to leave?"

"Heartbroken."

"All that discipline . . . " she murmured.

"All that power . . . "

"All gone . . . "

He sighed wistfully.

"Those were the days, Miss Jones."

"I'm sure they were, Mr Brown."

"There was this lad," he said. "Name of Seaton, or Heaton, or something. A cocky little lad, he was. Too clever by half. This was during National Service, when squaddies were often too clever by half. He'd got his School Cert, so he thought he should have been an officer. A clever little bleeder. Showed no respect. Used to wind me up, which was bad for my digestion."

He put a hand on his stomach, to show her where Seaton wound him up.

"He was book-clever, but he wasn't life-clever. And he certainly wasn't prison-clever. A pretty boy like that shouldn't let himself get sent down."

He grinned at the wall.

"He was the prettiest tart on C block. Everyone was after him, but he was straight, he wasn't having any. So one evening we shoved him in solitary. Away from his mates. Let him stew a bit. That night we let five Argyll and Sutherlands go in there. Rest and recreation for the lads."

He picked up one of the beer-mats and looked at the hunting scene it showed.

"Just imagine, Miss Jones. Five hairy jocks. One after the other."

"Must have taught him not to wind you up," she said.

"I think it did," he said.

"Weren't you worried you might bump into him on the outside?"

"Not really."

"After he was released, I mean. Once he'd done his time and left."

"Seaton-Heaton left feet first, Miss Jones."

He glanced at the clock above the fireplace.

"Seaton-Heaton was a flyer."

He examined the cork underside of the mat.

"Seaton-Heaton took a dive off the third-floor landing."

He slammed the beer-mat down on the table. The glasses jumped.

"He fell, Miss Jones. He fell for Queen and Country."

The barman looked up. Someone coughed in the corner. She wanted to spew.

"And now you know the nature of the beast, I suggest – as you put it earlier – that we do the deal."

She placed the folded-up *Guardian* on the shiny table-top. She rested her hand on the newspaper and felt the bulge of the money inside. He tilted his head to try and read the upside-down headline. It said something about secrecy and defence contracts and computers. *Guardian* headlines tend to be verbose.

"I hope you're not a *Guardian* reader, Miss Jones."

"Would it bother you if I were, Mr Brown?"

"Things are really getting bad if I'm doing business with *Guardian* readers."

Such a nerveless face, he had, with his dead eyes and his scrubbed skin.

"What's wrong with them?"

"They whine, Miss Jones. They criticise. They complain. And they think they were born to rule."

"You don't like them, then."

"I'm not saying I don't like them," he said. "I'm just saying they get up my nostrils."

It was four in the afternoon. Up and down the land, in hostelries large and small, deals were being struck, fates sealed, lives bought, names deleted. In oak pubs and plastic pubs, pubs with muzak and pubs without, over brandies and warm beer, people were buying and selling, ducking and diving, making clammy little agreements and shaking on it and walking swiftly away. And it was so civilised, so European, so continental, not to have to meet on a park bench or under a bus shelter or beside a flyover. Whoever invented all-day opening, she was thinking, should be canonised.

What was he saying?

"Sorry, what were you saying?" she said.

"I was saying you might like to tell me what you want it for."

"What I want what for?"

"The goods, Miss Jones. I'd like to know why you need my goods. That's how I operate. How do you operate, Miss Jones?"

"I operate on the need-to-know principle, Mr Brown," she said, "and I'm afraid you don't need to know."

He drained the rest of the Scotch and pressed his moist lips together.

"I'd like to give you some free advice, Miss Jones."

"Fire away." She sipped her Babycham. "No pun intended."

"Whatever you're going to do, don't hang on to the goods longer than necessary. The number's been removed, so it can't be traced. More to the point, it can't be traced to me. That's how I like it, and that's how I intend to keep it."

He ran a finger round the rim of the glass.

"Don't handle it without wearing gloves. Don't walk around with the safety catch off. Don't point it unless you're prepared to use it, and don't use it unless you know you'll get away with it."

"Anything else?"

"Yes," he said. "Don't blame me if you get caught."

"I won't get caught."

He shrugged. It wasn't his concern. He was clean, anyway. He reached across and slid the newspaper towards him. He slipped a hand between the pages and began counting money.

"It's soggy," he muttered.

"A soggy profit is better than none."

"It's a pleasure doing business with you, Miss Jones."

"I know it is."

"Okay," he said, after a couple of minutes. He removed his hand. It was black with printer's ink. He refolded the paper and tucked it under his arm. She put a hand on his elbow, as if they were lovers.

"Aren't we forgetting something?"

"Trust me, Miss Jones."

90

She followed him out of the bar and through the double doors and on to the forecourt. He walked over to his car, which gleamed yellow under a tungsten lamp. He put his key in the lock and turned it and opened the door.

"Time to say farewell, Miss Jones."

He swung himself down into the driver's seat. If this was a sting it had been quite a neat sting. She'd give him that. She'd also give him something else, if they ever met again.

For a second time that night, she watched him wind down the window and poke his head out.

"There's a litter bin at the back of the car park," he said. "You delve down deep enough and you'll find it in a Waitrose carrier bag. There's one clip of ammo. It's an Italian automatic and the safety's on the left, just above the trigger."

He put the car into gear.

"I've never seen you before, I'm not seeing you now, and I don't want to see you again."

She watched him swing out of the exit, together with her four hundred.

She turned round and let her eyes scan the forecourt. There were two litter bins. She walked towards the one that was in darkness. Be quick now, Bella. She walked up to the bin and jammed her hand down like she was always poking around in the rubbish, as if it was something she did every day. She'd always been lucky with the Lucky Dip.

When she was five, she'd plunged her hand into a tub of sand at the school fair, and pulled out the nicest toy they'd hidden inside. The sun had shone and the grass was green and everyone smiled down at her because she was only five, and she was the one who won the nicest toy they put in the tub.

And her tiny heart, her tiny toddler's heart, overflowed with love for the world because the world was full of prizes and you only had to shut your eyes and you could pluck them out of the sand.

She kept her eyes open this time. She kept her eyes open and tried to look normal as she brought out empty cigarette packets and greasy crisp bags and apple cores and a woollen glove and a used condom. You bloody deviant, Brown. She fished deeper. Nothing. Thieving pederast, I'll get you.

Her hand went deeper still and her fingers touched the metal base. Nothing there. She needed to hold it in her hand. She needed to clasp her warm fingers around the cold barrel and feel its dead weight in her hand. She had to hold it in her hand.

You bastard, Brown. You bloody catamite. You lying piece of degenerate garbage. And when she thought that all was lost, when she thought she'd burst and bellow with her need, she stretched and touched and – God is Great – she found her holy grail. She felt the smooth, familiar plastic and the hard lump inside. She lifted out the carrier and without waiting, without probing further, without tempting fate any longer, walked swiftly out into the street.

# CHAPTER ELEVEN

You know how it is when you need to have a man? When you get the sudden urge to put your arms around a man? When the heat gets too hot, and you're burning for a man?

That's how she was on Saturday night.

She had the need. She had the urge. And she had the heat. She had it so bad she was burning. She went out hot in the snow-cold night, and she wondered if they knew when they watched her. She wondered if they knew, by the glow in her eye, that she had it so bad she was burning.

She walked like a witch down Marine Parade. Her high heels clicking on the ice-covered pavement. Her cheap cotton coat, and her red satin dress, and her sheer silk, slut-black stockings.

It's half-past ten on a Saturday night. She's going past the discos on Marine Parade. Her thin summer coat blown open by the wind. They see the scarlet dress underneath. The wind off the sea blows her summer coat open, and they shudder at the dress underneath.

She's getting all the glances as she walks down the road. The glances that you get if the wind blows your coat, and they see what you wear on a Saturday night. The glances that you get if you walk down the road, with the wind in your hair on a Saturday night. The glances that you get if you're out on your own, and your high heels are tapping on a Saturday night.

She's begging for it. Just begging for it. They'll tell you, if you ask them: she's begging for it. The whore-faced slutbitch is spinning down the road. She's spinning down the road and she's smiling to herself. She's out on her own on a Saturday night, and they choke on their beer as they watch her go by.

She's out on her own in a seaside resort, in a thin summer coat which is whipped by the wind. And she's burning so much that she can't feel the cold. She's burning so much she's afraid she'll combust. She's burning with yearning to be with a man.

She went past a club where they stood by the door. They watched her walk by in her wine-coloured dress. They saw the red dress and they called her a slag. She made them see red, so they said what they said. They called her a slag as she went down the road. She heard what they said, and she kept on going. It burst in her head, but she kept on going.

Mad dogs go out in the midday sun. Slags go out at night. They stood and watched her receding back. They called her a slag as they stood by the door. They called her a slag, and she heard what they said, and it burst in her head, but she kept on going down Marine Parade.

They came so close that Saturday night. They didn't even know how lucky they were. How lucky they were that she kept on going. They saw what they thought was just scrag off the street. A smirk-faced slut. A piece of meat. They didn't see her eyes as she kept on going. The mad-dog eyes as she kept on going. Burning down the road, spinning down the road, grinning down the road on a Saturday night.


When she was finished, they'd try to find a plan. They'd try to find a pattern. They'd piece together all the things she'd done, and try to make them fit. She'd have to let them know that they really shouldn't bother. She'd have

94

to let them know that they shouldn't waste their time.

There wasn't any plan. There wasn't any pattern. They couldn't make it fit. There wasn't any meaning, if you weren't that way inclined.

Everything was random. Everything was pointless. The only point was to damp down the burning. And even that was pointless: she'd damped it down the night before, and it had flared up once again.

Even the hotel she chose. They'd think: why *that* hotel? She'd shrug and say: why not?

She walked through a gilded foyer. It was one of the better sort of hotels. The sort that charges extra for breakfast. Muted colours and subdued voices and a piano tinkling in the corner. She caught her reflection in an antique mirror. An entrancing sight. A vision of lurex loveliness. Bella was in her glad-rags.

She had scooped and smeared and gently massaged. She had powdered and shaded and highlighted. She had painted herself, transformed herself, reinvented herself, until she became their most fertile fantasy. A dark-eyed siren from the deep. The Lilith of their dreams.

She touched her belly with her fingers. The laced-up corset held her tight. Tighter than any man could hold her. She smiled at her glorious image, for she knew what she knew: no-one would ever love Bella, the way Bella loved Bella.

She entered the bar. Bella is here. Bella has arrived. She sank on to a leather stool and smiled at the barman. Such a pretty boy. Cherubic, almost. He brought her vodka, with ice and lemon, the way she always likes it.

She hoped the manager wouldn't see her. She always thought of Joey, when she saw a hotel manager. She hated scenes, and managers made scenes. They were always making scenes when they saw her.

In the good old days, when Bella was bad, before she went mad, the managers would have her dragged out. They'd have her dragged out like a piece of rank trash.

And the tears. Such tears she shed. The tears that she wept when she came down the steps. And Joey in his car. Her protector and defender. Her teacher and tormentor.

He liked it so much that he laughed as she cried. He had a song he used to sing: You got above your station, and your station's King's Cross. He lost a lot of money, but he still found it funny.

She nodded to the slim-hipped cherub, and he fixed her another. Brazen little Bella, drinking on her own. The little hussy. The little trollop.

"Make that two," a voice said. A voice that carried. Not a murmuring voice. You'd think he was somebody, with a voice like that.

He sat down on the next stool. His plump thigh pressed against her. An odour of perspiration enveloped the bar.

"I'm Norman," he said.

"Hello, Norman." She held the glass to her lips. "I'm Bella."

He put an olive in his mouth.

"Are you waiting for someone, Bella?"

She turned to look at him. He had a large, square head. A bald and sweating head. A Prussian-looking head. She wouldn't want to give birth to a head like that. The nativity of Norman could not have been nice.

"No-one," she said. "No-one in particular."

His piggy eyes were watching her. Sliding up and down in a quick, fluid movement. Taking in the hair, the dress, the promise.

"I hope you don't mind," he said. "You look so appealing in that lovely red dress. I hope you don't mind my joining you."

"Not at all."

"You've got no special plans for the evening?"

"I'm just killing time."

The barman set down their drinks. Norman slid hers across.

"Let's kill it together."

96

"Yes," she said. She fished out the lemon. "Let's."

He had a brown suit and wide hips. She's never liked brown. She likes black suits, or navy suits, or grey suits. She hates brown suits. He could have worn a different suit, but he couldn't help his hips. His hips were so wide, he could have had children. Magnificent, childbearing hips. When a man has hips as wide as those, you know for sure he's a thinking man.

"Are you here on holiday?"

"I live here."

"A local! How fascinating. Do they call you Brighton Bella?"

She smiled. The demureness of her smile.

"Not yet."

"I'm down here for a conference," he said. "Academic seminar. Clinical psychology, but I won't bore you with all the gory details. It's far too tedious. You're far too pretty. I won't try and bore you with all the details."

She was in the presence of an intellectual. A man who moved in the world of ideas. A man who, in idle moments, toyed not just with himself, but with Great Thoughts.

When intellectuals spend the night together, they do not merely rub bodies. They rub minds. They pause, mid-orgasm, to ponder the finer points of Friedmanite economics. They have brains of huge proportions, which pulse and throb with interesting insights.

She was in the presence of an intellectual, and when she hears the word intellectual, she reaches for her gun.

"Are you a professor, Norman?"

"Yes," he said.

He drained his glass.

"Sort of."

"What's a sort-of professor, Norman?"

"Someone who *should* have been professor. Someone who, but for the cuts, *would* have been professor. A sort-of professor, my exquisitely inquisitive young lady, is a professor in all but name."

"I see," she said.

She could have let it drop. She'd touched him on a tender spot, she knew. And it's not as if it matters either way. She's not a snob about such things. But she thought she'd like to get it straight.

"So you *are* a professor?"

He looked irritated.

"I'm not *quite* a professor. I'm *almost* a professor."

"So you're *not* a professor?"

"If you want to be *precise*, if you want to be *exact*, if you want to be *pedantic* – no, I'm *not* a professor. I'm a senior lecturer, at the top of the scale, which is *virtually* a professor."

"I didn't know that, Norman."

"Well now you do."

She sucked on the lemon.

"I'm glad we've cleared that up, Norman."

He was rapidly working his way through the olives. They were big, black and juicy.

"Not for me, thanks," she said. Rather superfluously.

The ashtray began to fill up with stones.

"And what's your field, then?" he asked, between bites.

"I'm in sanitation."

"Oh."

"I sanitise."

"You're not one of those women who wears dungarees and goes out on dustcarts, are you?"

"I'm more in the executive line."

He looked relieved.

"You mean you make the decisions."

"That's right. First you decide, then you execute your decisions."

"Something like a consultant?"

"Something like that."

"Must be fairly demanding."

"It is, Norman. Fairly demanding is what it is."

A spurt of juice escaped from his mouth as he chewed the last remaining olive.

"You don't actually *enjoy* dealing with refuse, though." He wiped his oily lips with a handkerchief. "Surely not."

"It's funny you should ask that, Norman, because I think I do. The trouble is, people get so used to the dirt they forget it's there. And that's a big mistake. That's a very big mistake. You let the rubbish pile up, and sooner or later it'll take over. If you don't control the garbage, the garbage will control you."

"I must say you sound incredibly *dedicated*."

"I am, Norman. Incredibly. It's more of a vocation, really. A kind of calling. I feel I've been called to clean up the mess."

"A sort of one-woman crusade?"

"A holy war." She sipped her drink. "And I take no prisoners."

They both laughed at little Bella's little joke.

He ordered another round, and winked at the barman. He doesn't know that it clears her head. The more she drinks the better she thinks.

She hadn't chosen him. She hadn't picked him out, put the mark on his forehead, said you'll be the one. She hadn't plucked him out against his will. She hadn't dragged him from the line with her nails in his crotch. She hadn't said: bad luck, you're wearing brown.

She'd just sat by herself on a leather stool, wrapped in her deep red dress. And he'd come to her. He'd found her. He'd said: me, me, me! It has to be me! Dog-like, lemming-like he'd come to her. He'd come with his square head and his wide hips and he'd sat down beside her.

It didn't have to be him. It could have been anyone. It could have been any of them, with their thick wallets and their whisky breath and their strutting, rutting walk. It could have been any one of them who'd seen her by the bar and nearly made their move.

She would have taken any one of them, had he only asked. She would have gladly gone with any one of them. She would have given any one of them all she had to give.

99

But he'd been the one. He'd seen her and he wanted her. And he was going to have her.

"Are you married, Norman?"

"Separated, thank God."

"I suppose your wife didn't understand you."

"She neither understood, nor cared. A very cold woman. I tried to help her as much as I could. I tried to encourage her to better herself. Educationally, I mean. Not that it matters, but it would have helped her self-esteem. I think her basic problem was her low self-esteem."

"I think you're probably right."

"She wasn't stupid. I'm not saying she was stupid. I wouldn't have married her if I thought she was stupid. But she wasn't what you'd call a terribly *perceptive* woman. She didn't have what you'd call an original *mind*. Shallow was what she was. Intellectually shallow. I thought she should be told, so I told her."

"That was very truthful of you, Norman."

"But she wouldn't accept it. She wouldn't face up to it. Oh *no*, not *her*. An emotional cripple was what she called me, believe it or not. A very childish woman. A very childish, spiteful woman."

"Women can be so cruel . . . "

"Oh I know," he said, "I know. But I'm *sorry* for her, more than anything. It's sad when you try and help someone and they're not even grateful. She used to say that I was trying to undermine her, but of course the lacuna in that argument was that there was nothing there to undermine."

"The what . . . ?"

"Sorry?"

"The what in the argument?"

"Oh. The lacuna. The hole."

"Lacuna means hole?"

"So they say."

She stared in wonder.

"That's interesting, Norman."

She listened to him as he carried on talking. She was

100

a good listener. She's always been a good listener. She watched his lips as they formed the words, and she watched the words as they came out of his mouth. He was a thinking man who used a lot of words. He was a very wordy man.

"I'm very particular about women, Bella. Always have been. Always will be. They have to have very pronounced human qualities. I think that's the most important thing, in the final analysis. Their human qualities. I put my women on a pedestal. I worship them. I'd do anything for them. Call me old-fashioned, if you will."

"You're old-fashioned, Norman."

He squeezed her hand. Her stomach heaved.

"I can tell you're a deeply caring woman, Bella. It's so unusual to meet such an attractive woman, who's also such an obviously caring woman. There can't be many of you about."

"I don't believe there are."

"It's wonderful to meet a really warm, earthy, appreciative woman. A womanly woman."

The sweat from his scalp was running down past his ears and dripping off his chin. Just looking at him reminded her how hot she was. She was weak from the heat. The heat and the smoke were making her eyes water. If you didn't know her better, you'd have thought she was weeping.

"It's hot in here," she said. "I can't take the heat."

"Shall we go outside? It's cool outside."

"Too noisy," she said. "I can't take the noise."

He touched her tenderly on the cheek.

"You're a very special person," he said. "A very warm, sensitive, special person. I knew that as soon as I saw you. Take it from me. It takes one to know one. You've got human qualities. Deeply human qualities. I could write a poem about your human qualities."

Again he placed a moist hand over hers.

"I think we should go up to my room. Nothing expected, nothing intended. We can stand on the balcony and gaze at

101

the sea. Share a moment of quiet communion in the midst of life's hurly-burly."

"You're inviting me upstairs?"

Oh, rash, rash Norman. Foolish twerp. Be it on your own bonce.

"We've both suffered, you and I. We've suffered for our softness. We've suffered for our gentleness. I want to take you in my arms and soothe away the suffering, but it's too soon, I know. I make no demands of you. I ask only that you come with me to my room, and stand beside me on the balcony. Only that."

He released her hand.

"You want it too," he said, "I can tell."

Her hand felt damp. She wanted to wipe his wetness off her hand. She'd use a tissue. Then screw it up. Then drop it in his drink. She wanted to soak the film of sweat from his face with twin-ply kitchen paper. She wanted to wring him out like a rag, and chuck him in the bin.

He gazed at her with deep devotion.

"To stand together, arm in arm . . . "

"Sounds quite sublime," she said.

He took her elbow as she stepped down from the stool. The chivalry of a Norman. The gallantry.

The other drinkers watched them leave. The salesmen. The delegates. The boys away from home. They looked at her with mild distaste. Their thoughts were plain to see: We know what you are. We know what you are, and what you've got to offer. It didn't have to be him. Any one of us could have taken what you're giving.

And she stared them out with a cold, bored stare. She walked right past and stared them out: You're lucky men. It didn't have to be him. It could have been one of you. Any one of you could have got what he'll be getting.

You're lucky men, believe me. You don't know what I am, and you wouldn't want to take what I'll be giving.

# CHAPTER TWELVE

They took the lift to the third floor. He led her down the corridor, and stopped outside Room 23. He unlocked the door and pushed it open and let her go in front of him. He came in after her. She could feel his closeness in the dark. A switch clicked.

"Let there be light."

You could see why he'd almost made professor.

She liked the room. She liked its anonymity. She liked the way it could have been any room. In any hotel. It didn't have to be Room 23, Hotel Samara.

"I'll just put on something more comfortable," he said, unbuttoning his shirt. The fat of his neck flopped over his collar. She thought it suited him.

"Would you like to stand on the balcony while I get changed?" He was scratching himself vigorously through the string vest.

She stepped out through the french windows and he drew the curtain behind her. It was one of those thin, narrow balconies, with an ornamental guard-rail. They call them Juliet balconies. She looked across at Palace Pier, with its coloured lights winking against the night sky. The odours of candyfloss and burgers and fried chicken wafted up to her.

103

The pier jutted into the sea, but the sea was invisible. You couldn't see it and you couldn't smell it. That's the trouble with Brighton. That's one of Brighton's troubles. Brighton smells so much itself, that sometimes you can't smell the sea, even when you're so close you could spit in it.

She heard voices approaching down the street. Loud, proud, beery voices. Saturday-night-out-with-the-lads voices.

"You wanker, give that back."

"Eat shit."

"My mum bought me these boots."

"You can see Crawley from my bedroom window."

"Fucking nuns. I fucking hate nuns."

"Nice motor."

"I've *done* Risley. Risley's a *doddle*."

"So I said to her: we can do this the easy way, or the hard way. Either way is my way."

There are five of them, and they've got that maggoty way of seeming to be everywhere at once. Leaping over dustbins, and drumming on car roofs, and moving down the road with that straddle-legged walk to show that they're big brave boys and Brighton belongs to them.

"This place is dead."

"Shame there's no Pakis."

"She couldn't walk for three days afterwards."

And as they went beneath her, she experienced, for the first time in her life, a pang of purest penis-envy. She knew, as she watched them pass below, that a willy would indeed have been wonderful. For she was unable, anatomically incapable, of expressing herself in the way that she wished.

She could only imagine what it would be like to stand on the balcony and empty her bladder. To urinate on the low-life slinking past. To send a graceful parabola of piss streaming down on to their bovine heads. To wash them in her holy waters, and wish them luck as she waved them goodbye.

104

She sighed and went back into a darkened room, closing the curtains behind her. Mustn't grumble, she told herself. Look on the bright side. Make the best of what you've got. (Homely homilies have always helped her.)

A table-lamp flicked on.

Norman was standing by the bed.

He possessed the most hairless torso she'd ever seen on a post-pubescent male. His body had a plucked, waxed, defoliated look, as if it only remained to baste him in melted butter, and pop him into the oven at gas mark 6 with an apple in his mouth.

She had once read an article on cannibalism. Two thousand words in a quality paper about the culinary habits of Papua New Guinea. Two thousand words on the real reason they do it. The mystery behind the heathen mess they leave on their tablecloths.

The point of it all is not, it seems, to devour the enemy. The point lies not in biting off his best bits, chewing them up with jacket potato, then burping quietly and licking your greasy lips.

The point of cannibalism, its essential core, is not really to eat your enemy at all, but to languidly search for a shady spot, then squat down in the grass and excrete your enemy.

She could see there was a certain logic to it. A certain organic, biodegradable, additive-free wholesomeness to that kind of staple diet. It was one way of achieving self-sufficiency, one way of weaning yourself off the dependency culture. A sort of waste-not, want-not approach to those you'd probably never liked much, anyway.

But while the thought of Norman being consumed, digested and transformed into gently steaming turds had its superficial appeal, Bella has always been finicky about her food. Refinement has always marked her table manners. Even a Bella has her limits. Let the dogs die in peace. She might beat them, but she would never eat them.

She watched him as he moved around the room. He kept slapping his hairless chest, like a Sumo wrestler, sending sprays of golden sweat into the air. Pink and mottled skin was stretched like sausage over mounds of minced flesh. Barely a hair hung under his arms. Only a few brown tufts around his nipples competed with the darker growth that embraced his pudenda, such as they were. Indeed, his lack of self-consciousness was extraordinary, given what he'd been given. There was nothing wrong, she'd always felt, with a few healthy inhibitions.

The nonchalance with which his generous breasts lay on that swollen belly momentarily unnerved her. She would have killed for a pair like that. When he turned to check he'd locked the door, she saw the bleak white tundra of his buttocks, and she could have wept for womankind.

And then something happened to her. Something so horrid and so beastly that she would recall it, ever after, with nauseated disbelief.

To her abiding remorse and eternal shame, she began to feel the merest twinge of desire, the faintest suggestion of kindled passion. For she too has needs. She too has urges. She too has lubricious longings that must be assuaged.

But why him? she demanded of her treacherous labia, as the glistening blob rolled towards her. Why him, you libidinous layabouts?

And why not? came the slightly peeved reply.

And so it came to pass that Bella, who had held herself back for so long and had willingly forgone so much, kicked off her panties and bent over the bed. She rolled up the dress and closed her eyes and waited, salivating in spite of herself, for Norman's lurching entry.

Two plump hands grabbed her hips. Fat thighs forced her legs apart. Something moist and spongy pressed against her privates. He rubbed it up and down. He rubbed it round and round. He moaned and groaned. He cursed and prayed. But all to no avail. Her gaping nether regions felt as though crisscrossed by the drunken meanderings of a garden snail.

"Nearly there," he coaxed. "Nearly there, Percy. Good lad. Easy does it. Up we go, Perce."

106

But Percy remained in his slug-like state. He didn't care. He wasn't bothered. He couldn't give a toss. He wouldn't be browbeaten, and he wouldn't be bribed. Percy remained impervious.

Minutes passed.

Bella waited. Bella was patient. Bella understands.

And then, with boredom beginning to grip, when she was about to ring room service for a nice cup of cocoa, she felt Percy insinuate himself into her crevice. He seemed to like his new habitat, for he began – slowly yet undeniably – to grow. The slug gradually became a reptile. Norman's breath burst from his lips in a sob of gratitude.

"Yes, yes. That's it. Oh God. Oh Mother. Oh Percy. Just a bit more. Just a bit more. Nearly there. Yes, yes. Nearly there. You can do it. Yes, yes. Oh, no. Oh, Perce. Don't go. Not yet. No, no . . . "

But Norman's penis was a bolshy penis. A singularly obtuse and stubborn penis. It was content to rest lightly in her crease and observe proceedings through its unblinking, slitty eye. And Norman, man of action that he was, began to rub it ever more desperately against her.

Bella frowned at the patterned duvet. What on earth was going on back there? What disgusting perversion was he trying to perpetrate twixt her sullen cheeks? She ducked her head and stared back through her thighs. All she could see was his wrinkled scrotum, his little sack of goodies, bobbing about in a bemused sort of way. Norman grunted as Percy resumed his burrowings. She was having none of that.

"Not in *there*, you berk. In the *lacuna!*"

Perhaps it was the harsh note in her voice, perhaps it was his own world-weariness, his sense of cosmic alienation. Whatever it was, Percy dwindled, Percy shrank, Percy failed to persevere.

She felt the thing being lifted away, soft and clammy as a melted suppository. She heard him step back, and she straightened up and put a hand to her aching neck. Thank you *very* much, Norman. That *was* educational. If

107

photographers do it in the dark, and surfers do it standing up, academics obviously don't do it at all.

She turned round to face him, and couldn't help but gaze down at the guilty party. Percy was quietly dribbling. Priapic he wasn't. But neither was he entirely limp. He seemed to be in the throes of a profound identity crisis, confused, bewildered, unsure whether to go north or south. He was neither fish nor fowl, neither stiff nor spent, neither one thing nor the other. One of the floating voters of the penile world.

"I'm so sorry," she said. "I really am."

She shook her head regretfully.

"Better to have tried and failed, than not to have tried at all," she said. "I suppose."

Norman held the offending and offensive object between thumb and forefinger. He didn't look a happy man. Norman needed to be comforted. Norman expected to be comforted. Norman was touchingly confident of being comforted.

"Actually . . . " he began.

"Yes, Norman?"

His fat little lecturer's grin was half-bashful and half-brazen.

"Failure to achieve erection isn't that important, as it happens."

"Says who?"

"My therapist."

"But he would, though, wouldn't he?"

There is a certain etiquette to be observed on such occasions. A certain protocol. Certain mutual reassurances that are lovingly and lyingly exchanged to soothe wounded pride and rebuild broken egos. The post-droop diplomacy that is the sex war carried on by other means.

He must not imply that he found her unattractive, and was therefore unable to perform. And she must not suggest that he might prefer to stick to self-abuse.

These are the rules. And they are not arbitrary rules. They are not random rules. They are rules grounded in what each fears most, the most devastating thing a man might suffer from a woman, or a woman from a man.

He fears her ridicule. She fears his rage. She might laugh at him. He might kill her.

There is no balance in the fear. There is no balance in the terror. Justice demands balance. Balance demands Bella.

So when she could no longer control the twitching of her mouth, and threw back her head and exploded with a laughter so huge it seemed to buffet the walls, he reared back in shock and horror, as if she were a foul heretic who had just denied the divinity of Jehovah.

She sank to her knees and the laughter gusted out of her in mad peals and endless gales. She held her sides and rocked to and fro and tears of joy poured from her eyes. She laughed, and her laughter was a terrible sin. It was sinful laughter.

You must never laugh. Whatever they do, don't laugh. Whatever they don't do, don't laugh. And never, ever laugh when you're in a hotel room with a stranger. Even if he's an educated stranger, with small feet and large hips. Whatever you do, don't laugh.

Unless you're Bella.

If you're Bella, you can break all the rules. If you're Bella, and the adrenalin's pumping, you can throw back your head and point your finger and mock the phallic god that failed.

But only if you're Bella, if you're mad, bad Bella and you're burning up inside.

# CHAPTER THIRTEEN

When the heel of the shoe he held in his hand smashed into her mouth, it sent her spinning backwards on to the carpet. It was one of those expensive leather brogues that someone who hasn't quite made professor is inclined to wear. She put a hand to her face and felt the split lip. He's drawn blood. Her lip is bleeding.

And why not? Does not a Bella bleed?

She looks up at him and wonders if he will kill her now. She wouldn't mind. It's not that she'd mind. She knows that one day someone will kill her. She knows that one day someone will have to kill her. It's not that she's not ready for it, or doesn't expect it, or can't face it.

But not now. Now is not the time. This is not the place. Norman is not the man. A Norman could never kill a Bella.

She smiles at him. Her mollifying smile. She smiles and makes her eyes crinkle with sincerity. Norman must be soothed. Norman must be placated. Norman must be nurtured, before he can be neutered.

She held up her hand and he lifted her to her feet.

"I'm sorry," she said. "Truly I am."

The contrition of Bella. What heart would not melt?

He pulled her close to him and twisted her arms behind

her and pressed his mouth, his soft and rosebud mouth, his weak, wet, woman's mouth, against hers. She wanted to gag at the feel of him but he held her tight and chewed her tongue until they both tasted salt. He released her and his lips parted and he had her blood on his teeth. He put his mouth against her neck, and his groin against her belly, and murmured into her ear. Hot, damp breath in her ear.

"Had to teach you a lesson. Quickest learned, soonest mended. Spare the rod and you spoil the child. You know what I mean."

"I know what you mean."

The sweat was pouring from him. From his neck and his chin and his chest and his stomach, and from the backs of his legs. How can a man with no body hair sweat so much? Is that normal? Is Norman normal?

If he could only have saved the sweat, if he could have distilled it and bottled it and sold it as table wine, he would have been a wealthy man. Only once in each generation is a man born who can sweat like Norman sweated. Only once in a lifetime is one born who can perspire so profusely, and so selflessly.

You had to give him that. Credit where it's due. He knew how to sweat.

They both made mistakes, that night. Hers was to laugh at him. To laugh too loud and too long. His was not to kill her for it.

Because you can't bully Bella any more. You can't make her cringe any more. You have to kill her, or leave her be. To smash her mouth and split her lip is not enough, any more. Either wipe her out, or let her be.

But don't hurt her. Don't give her pain. Don't make her head throb and her jaw ache. Don't send her spinning back to the floor with the heel of your shoe, then bite her tongue and think she's yours.

Just finish her, if you get the chance. She won't mind. She'll understand. She'll even help you, if she likes you, in her ever-helpful way.

He said: I shouldn't have hit you. I don't hit women, unless they deserve it, and you deserved it. You provoked me, and so I hit you. Fair's fair. You made me do it. It's your fault. I believe in communication. I am a great communicator. I communicate every day. I believe in talking things through. I despise violence. Violence is despicable. You made me do something I despise. I'm going to hit you again, because of what you made me do.

And he hit her again on her open lip, and it opened even wider.

She said: I made you do it. It's my fault. Mine is the guilt. I provoked you. I deserved it. I made you do what you despise.

He said: We're beginning to communicate.

She said: I've damaged you. I've wounded you. I want to make it up to you.

He said: Play a game with me. I'll forgive you if you play a game with me.

She said: What game?

He said: The bondage game.

She watched his piggy eyes sink deep in his piggy face.

She said: I'll play any game but that game. I don't like that game.

He said: But you said you'd make it up to me.

She said: I said it, and I'll do it. Any way but that way. You mustn't tie me up. It's not my cup of tea.

He said: I don't want to tie you up. I am an educated man. I want you to tie *me* up.

She said: Do you really mean that?

He said: I really mean that.

She said: I think we're beginning to communicate.

He brought the chair from the corner to the centre of the room. The seat was green dralon and it had a high wooden back. It looked like a dining chair. He sat down on the dralon seat of the dining chair and folded his arms.

She removed his leather belt from the loops in the waistband of his trousers. The leather of his leather belt was

112

almost as good as the leather of his leather brogues. It was very supple leather, the sort of leather that lends itself to binding educated men.

He put his arms behind the high wooden back of the chair and crossed his wrists. The sweat of anticipation was running down his back. She bent down and bound the belt around his wrists.

"Tighter," he urged.

She wrapped the belt around again, and pulled it tight until he gasped.

"Thank you, Mistress."

She walked round and stood in front of him. He gazed at her adoringly. He worshipped her. He would have fallen to his knees and kissed her feet, had she not tied him so firmly to the chair. His excitement built up until he was hard. And as she watched him, saying nothing, his excitement became huge.

"Norman," she said, "you're enormous."

"I know," he moaned, "I know. Do something. Please do something. Just do something quickly."

"Am I forgiven, Norman?"

"Yes, Mistress."

"Do you give me absolution?"

"Yes, Mistress."

"I'm going to gag you, Norman."

"Please," he murmured, "oh, please . . . " His eyes rolled back in his head. Norman was in a state of exaltation.

She picked up his off-white polyester shirt from the floor. "You've been a naughty boy, Norman."

"I know, I know! Norman's been a very naughty boy."

"What shall I do, Norman?"

"Punish me, Mistress. Teach me not to be a naughty boy."

"You're sure about that, Norman?"

"Punish me! Punish me!"

He tugged at his bonds in agitation. Both Norman and Percy, she realised, were in a highly emotional state.

"All right, Norman. I'll punish you — "

"Thank you, Mistress . . . "

" — but first I've got to go to the ladies". Won't be a tick."

He groaned.

"Hurry back," he breathed. "I can't wait forever."

She glanced at the quivering mass of jelly on the chair.

"You won't have to, Norman."

In the bathroom she removed the shower cap from its polythene bag, and filled the bag with ice-cold water from the cold-water tap. Then she pulled the chain, out of habit, and then she washed her hands, because the chain is always full of germs.

She came back into the room and stood behind him. His shirt was draped over her elbow, waitress-style. She leant over his shoulder and let the ice-cold water in the polythene bag splash down on to Norman's enormity.

"That's to teach you not to be a naughty boy," she said. "Now I'm going to teach you not to go with strange women."

She whipped the shirt around his yelling mouth, tying it by the sleeves.

"But before I do," she said, "before I do, I want to tell you something. I want to tell you something, Norman, and I want you to listen."

She flicked a piece of fluff from her sleeve.

"You revolt me, Norman. I mean that most sincerely. Every aspect of your being revolts me. Your body revolts me. Your attitudes revolt me. Your arrogance revolts me. Your stupidity revolts me. Your touch revolts me. And your sweat revolts me. I find you, in a word, revolting."

She leant forward to check the gag was tight.

"I'm going to kill you, Norman. I wasn't going to tell you, but I think you've got a right to know. You're going to die, Norman. You're going to die very soon. In this room. By my hand. You're going to die the death you deserve. It's going to be unpleasant for both of us, and we have to be strong."

His neck went puce as he tried to break the bonds he'd made her tie so tight.

114

"But I want you to understand that it's nothing personal. You're not going to die because you're you. You're not even going to die because you're revolting. If I killed everyone who revolts me, there wouldn't be many people left. So what I'd like to impress on you, Norman, before I send you off on your final sabbatical, is that you're going to die because you're unlucky. You're unlucky because the rules have changed, and nobody let you know."

Alas, poor Norman. The trouble with academics is that they're so used to their intimate little bistro dinners, where the bill gets split down the middle and they get fellated for free afterwards, that they forget that in the real world you have to pay. In the real world, where real women try to sell you the only real commodity they have, you always have to pay.

"It didn't have to be you, Norman. You didn't have to be the one. But you asked for it. You brought me here. You let me into your room. You shouldn't have done that, Norman. You shouldn't have let me squeeze past you into your room. Mummy should have warned you, Norman. She should have warned you not to take chances.

"You took a chance, Norman. You took a chance and you hit me with your shoe. You gave me pain, Norman. You hit me in the mouth and you gave me pain. I don't like pain. I have a very low pain threshold. Pain is not something I seek in life. I try to avoid pain. And now you're going to pay for my pain.

"You're going to pay for the pain you gave me, and you're going to pay for all the pain you've ever given.

"No, don't cry, Norman. I want you to be philosophical about this. Death comes to us all. Sooner or later, it takes us all. You're just being taken sooner."

Veins appeared on his neck and shoulders. They forced their way through the fat and gristle and popped up on his skin. Long-forgotten muscles banded together in a last vain attempt to jerk free of the belt that bound him.

"Be brave, Norman. And don't feel abandoned. Don't feel

you're the only one. You aren't the first, and you won't be the last."

And she shook the remaining droplets from the polythene bag and pulled it over his head, making sure not to tear it, careful to cover his air-holes. Then she walked round to face him, for some people feel threatened if you stand behind them.

"You've heard of foreplay," she said. "This is called afterplay."

Norman must have gone swimming in his younger years. The swimming must have developed his lungs. His lungs proved to be large lungs, which needed to suck in a lot of air. Barely a minute had passed before the bag began to mist up. The skin of his face took on a bluish tinge. Or maybe purple. It was difficult to tell, through the misted-up polythene.

A chubby leg kicked out at her. Grace under pressure was not one of his virtues. She thought the thud of Norman and chair toppling to the floor would have brought people running, but no-one came. It was a hotel, after all, and used to business clients and their ways.

A drain-like gurgle suddenly came from him, and a familiar stench filled the room. She wrinkled up her nose. Anal-retentive he obviously wasn't. The chambermaid would not be pleased.

She knelt down on the carpet. The polythene stuck to his face like a second skin. It was inside his gag-wedged mouth. It clung like cling-film to his bulging eyes. She peered closer and saw that one was brown, and the other green. That's unusual, she thought. A frog's croak escaped from his throat, and he was gone. He had perspired. He had expired.

Her lip was swollen, but she felt she should say some few words over the lifeless body. It seemed the decent thing to do.

She patted the top of his polythened head.

"Toodlepip, old bean," she said.

116

# CHAPTER FOURTEEN

She didn't sleep much on Saturday night. Sleep didn't
sneak up and steal her away. She lay wide-eyed in the
dark. Undressed, derobed, ensconced between the sheets,
sleep eluded her on Saturday night.

Poor Norman. She cooked his goose. She did him in.
She sent him for an early bath. The articles he'd written,
the papers he'd marked, the committees he'd graced, the
letters he'd signed, the books inside him, the glory before
him. All gone. Poor Norman.

But he really shouldn't have hit her. He shouldn't have
struck her on the mouth. He shouldn't have made her bleed,
for like many women, she cannot bear the sight of her own
blood.

He shouldn't have smashed her in the mouth. He
shouldn't have split her rose-red lip. He did it not because
she laughed, but because she was weaker, yet had dared
to laugh. If you think someone's weaker, you can split
their lip. If you think they're stronger, you join in the
joke.

He thought he'd got her measure. He thought – this
intellectual, this learned man, this bookophile – he thought
he'd slap her down, the way you'd slap a flea. Trust Norman
not to know. The educated idiot. The cultivated cretin. The

well-read fool who rushed right in. Trust Norman not to know the way she was.

Perhaps she'd over-reacted. But then again, perhaps not. Retribution had been required. She had been cruel to be kind. She had taught him an invaluable lesson: he who lives by the fist shall die by the polythene bag.

But all the same, Bella felt uncomfortable. Bella felt troubled. Her tooth was troubling her. If her tongue brushed the tooth, pain knifed up her cheek. If she moved her head, pain pierced her jaw. If she opened her mouth, pain slipped inside. If she closed her mouth, pain set up camp.

He'd given her a lot of pain. If she'd known how much pain he was going to give her, she wouldn't have let him off so lightly. If she'd known she wouldn't sleep that night, she'd have let him linger a little longer.

She was too nice. She was just too nice. Niceness had always been her undoing. People take advantage of you, if you're nice. They hit you in the mouth with the heel of their shoe. They think they'll get away with it, because they know that you're nice.

A lot of the world's trouble is caused by nice people. If they weren't so nice, no-one would hit them. And if they didn't get hit, they wouldn't hit back. Which would be a good thing, because when a nice person hits back, she hits back hard.

It's like nuclear deterrence. If they know you can bomb *them*, they won't bomb *you* in the first place. But if you don't show it, they won't know it. So if you've got it, flaunt it.

Logically, she should wear a sign, saying: This woman is vicious. If attacked, she will retaliate.

But who would believe her? They'd think her a loony-woman, which is something she's not. Or at least an exhibitionist, which is something she might be. Or a pro-vocateuse, which is something she has become. They'd arrest her for causing a breach of the peace. They'd fine her for carrying an offensive weapon. They'd jail her for incitement.

This is what's known as a dilemma, and she found herself impaled on its horns. She has to let them know she'll hit back. It's only fair, if they know, and she likes to be fair.

She has to make them understand that she'll chop off the hand that would hurt her. She'll burn down their homes, smash up their cars, snuff out their lives. She'll rub their faces in their faeces and gaily walk away.

But she can't tell them. To tell them is to warn them, and to warn them is to arm them. This is her dilemma. This is the dilemma of a Bella, as she lies in bed and tries to sleep, post-Timbo, post-Norman, not quite post-coitus, with her tooth throbbing, and her jaw aching.

And what's the big deal about retaliation, anyway? What's the great big moral deal? Why limit herself? What's wrong with a pre-emptive strike, now and then? If there's one of you, and there's too many of them, sometimes you can't just retaliate. Sometimes you have to initiate.

Because she was lucky with Norman. And she knows she was lucky with Norman. Norman could have done her a deal of damage, if he'd been that way inclined. Norman could have wiped her out, if he'd had the sense. He could have blitzkrieged her, devastated her, obliterated her, if he'd had half a brain. She was very lucky with Norman.

That's the basic problem, when you're Bella. You haven't got much of a choice. You can't let them get too close. If they get too close, you've got no chance. If they get too close, you go under. Her mistake with Norman was to let him get too close.

She lay wide-eyed through the night.

She was walking the high-wire. She was putting one foot in front of the other, arms outstretched, swaying her way along a thin metal thread.

She doesn't look down. She'll fall, if she looks down. She'll see there's no safety net, and she'll lose her faith. She'll topple off her wire and plummet to the earth. She'll see there's no net, and she'll lose her nerve, and go plunging

119

to the earth. She'll whistle her way down, her mouth forced open by rushing air, and far below all the little people would grin and point and watch her drop. They'd all be gloating as she fell, ready to run forward with their scrapers and scrape her off the ground.

So she mustn't lose her balance. She mustn't let a sudden gust blow her away. She mustn't go giddy from the height. She mustn't stop believing she can reach the other side. She just has to keep her balance, keep her head, and keep believing.

She lay wide-eyed through the night, and was still awake, still troubled, and still in pain when dawn poked its grubby finger into the room.

It took a while to find a dentist. It took a while to find one who'd see her on a Sunday. There are five pages of dental surgeons in Brighton's Yellow Pages, and it took her hours to work her way laboriously down the list. Most of her calls went unanswered. You couldn't really blame them. Even a tooth-healer is entitled to a day of rest. Even a drawer of teeth can spend a day with his dear ones, should he have any.

She spent hours on the phone, letting it ring, until recorded messages cut in to tell the caller to try again on Monday. She could have tried the hospital, and allowed some pus-faced youth to enter her mouth. But when it comes to her teeth, if nothing else, she prefers an older man.

It was gone three when she finally got through to someone in Kemp Town. His name was Reginald Mire, and his surgery had an oblique view of the Marina.

"I shouldn't really have agreed to see you," he said. His tanned and hairy arms poked from a short-sleeved Nehru shirt.

"I'm incredibly grateful."

"I only popped in to check the accounts," he added.

"I've had such pain."

"Pain is good for the soul."

"I take your point," she said, seating herself on the padded black chair. She swung her feet up on to the footrest. He pumped the chair higher, then made the top tilt back until her feet were higher than her head. They should be banned, those chairs.

"Where's your assistant?"

"It's Sunday."

He fiddled with a tray of tools.

"Nursey doesn't come on Sunday."

He tied a surgical mask around his face, and pulled on rubber gloves. The probes were arranged from left to right, in order of size.

"You are a little madam," he murmured, "making me work on my day off."

She doesn't like dentists. She doesn't like their attitude. They always seem to have an attitude problem. The same attitude problem.

He picked up a middle-sized probe and held it in front of her. His eyes seemed to glitter above the mask, though it might have been the light.

She opened her mouth without being told, and let him prod her gums and tap her teeth. She tried not to flinch when he hurt her. He frowned when she flinched, and she didn't want to make him frown when he had his hand in her mouth.

He pushed the metal probe into the gap in her tooth, and she heard some small sound of protest come from her throat.

"That doesn't hurt, does it? Surely not."

He began to lever it backwards and forwards, gouging out a larger and larger space.

"Oh yes," he said, "there's definitely a cavity here. Oh yes. My word, you have been in the wars, haven't you? I don't know. You girls. If it's not one thing, it's another." He put the probe back on the tray.

"You've chipped a tooth." He peered down at the damage

121

through half-moon glasses. "How did it happen?"

"Someone hit me."

"That wasn't very friendly. I hope you hit him back."

His forehead was unusually dry. Flakes of dead skin floated gently down whenever he moved. He should cream his forehead. He should lubricate it every night. He should smooth some oily substance into that dry, dentist's brow.

"I'll put in a temporary filling for you." He pulled the overhead drill down to eye-level. She heard it begin its pneumatic whine, and watched the head vibrate.

"I'd like an injection," she mumbled, through the cotton wads he'd stuffed in her mouth. "And I'd prefer you to use the fast drill."

She watched his eyes dilate above the mask.

"If you wouldn't mind."

He bent down low with his scaly forehead near her face.

"You can't use the fast drill for this type of filling."

The mask ballooned as he spoke.

"And you don't need an injection."

She shut her eyes and he put the thing into the hole Norman had made. He drilled deeper and deeper, digging out a neat ditch, making the cavity even larger, scouring out a bit of Lebensraum in her upper left incisor. The drill sounded like a prop-driven aeroplane. It performed loops and figures of eight in her dentine. It was the slowest of slow drills, and it hurt like hell.

She mentally opened her little red book, and turned to a fresh page, inscribed Reginald. He'd been wrong about the injection. He'd been so wrong that she'd have to make a note of it. She put a black mark against his name.

This was her new system. It worked like the driving licence. Each infringement of her code earned an endorsement. (Verbal warnings had long proved ineffective.) One endorsement was unfortunate. Two was pushing your luck. Three, and you lost your licence. Three endorsements

122

meant a lifetime ban. She put the first black mark against his name. The drill stopped. She opened her eyes.

"That wasn't so bad," he pronounced, "was it now."

His hand passed in front of her and dropped a tablet into a glass of water. It fizzed and the water turned pink.

"Have a good rinse."

She swilled warm water around her mouth and spat into the sink. Seeing bits of tooth disappear down the plughole reminded her of Timmy and Norm. She rinsed her mouth and reminisced.

Timothy had earned an abundance of endorsements by the time he got sent down. But Norman had been unfortunate. She would have given him two, at most. It was Norman's misfortune to have met her in her pre-judicial phase. Justice for Norman had been perhaps too swift. A graffito was scrawled on her mental brick wall: Norman was Innocent, OK? Another appeared underneath: Too bad.

She lay back on the chair and let him fill the hole. He plugged it with white filling, scraped away the excess, stuffed in some more, scraped and plugged and scraped. He took away the probe and removed some filler from the tip and rolled it into a tiny ball and flicked it to the floor.

"That's that," he said. "All done."

"How temporary is a temporary filling?"

"Come back in a day or two. I might have to fit a crown. We'll see how it goes."

But Bella would be gone, in a day or two. Bella would have flown the coop. Bella would have done a bunk.

She rinsed out her mouth for a second time. The new filling felt rough against her tongue. The tooth still throbbed from the drill. She removed the plastic napkin from around her neck and he pumped the chair down.

"Thank you," she muttered. (The grudgingness of her gratitude.)

He pulled off his mask.

"My pleasure," he said.

She watched him cross to the sink by the wall. He turned on the tap and washed his hands.

"What do I owe you?"

"Let's see," he said. The hands disappeared beneath a grey-looking towel. "One large filling. Emergency private treatment. Let's call it fifty pounds."

She raised her eyebrows.

He shrugged.

"I don't like Sundays."

She took out her purse and unfurled five tenners. The Timbo fund was fast depleting. She was spending money like she had no tomorrow.

"How soon can I eat?"

"About twelve hours or so. Give or take."

"See you in a day or two, then," she said.

"Or thereabouts."

He pulled on a check sports jacket with leather elbow-patches. The Nehru collar looked strange underneath.

"No more patients today?"

"No more patients."

"That's nice," she said.

"It is."

"No more patients for Mr Mire," she said.

"Reginald."

"No more patients for Reginald."

"None," he said.

She slung the handbag over her shoulder.

"Have you got a brother called Ronald, Reginald?"

"Why should I have?"

"Ronnie and Reggie, Reginald. That's why."

"Before your time, I would have thought."

"Well before."

"What's your interest then?"

"We did them in Social Studies."

"Common thieves." He looked annoyed. "East-End riff-raff."

124

"The Criminal as Catalyst."

"Swaggering round London with their minders."

"I got a Grade A."

"Anyone can be a hero with a gun," he sneered. "Any little nobody can be somebody with a gun."

"I think you've hit the nail on the head there, Reginald."

"I like it when you say my name."

"Do you?"

"I do."

"Do all your patients call you Reginald, Reginald?"

"Only the private ones. Only the ones who pay. If they pay I let them use my name."

"It's certainly worth it, Reginald. It's well worth fifty pounds."

"It's vulgar to talk money. Nice girls shouldn't talk money."

"I'll tell you a secret, Reginald: nice girls *only* talk money."

"Are you a nice girl?"

"I'm a very nice girl."

"Would you like a lift?"

"A lift?"

"My car's outside. I could give you a lift."

"I thought you lived here."

"God, no. I just rent this place. I live in a West Sussex village."

She looked at his blondness. He was a very blond man.

"Rustic Reginald," she said.

She smiled at him. He didn't smile back. He was eyeing her hips.

"Which way are you heading?" he asked.

He could have been a Scot, he was so fair. He had sand-coloured hair, and sand-coloured eyebrows. Pale grey eyes like his pale grey towel. He could have been a Highlander, but his accent was pure Highbury.

"Brunswick area."

"No problem."

He didn't tidy his equipment. He didn't put anything

in anything for a sterilising soak. He just left it for Nursey, and held the door open and followed her out to the street. Men were often opening doors for her, these days.

The car was a stunning Mercedes CE. Midnight blue, black leather seats, and automatic. She was always wary of men who drove automatics. She couldn't help wondering what they they did with their spare hand.

But the music was good. Sibelius soared out from the compact disc player. Culture, she thought, approvingly. She was very partial to a bit of culture. He touched the throttle and the car surged forward. Her tooth still hurt.

They turned right on to Madeira Drive and purred up to the Palace Pier roundabout. He drove across and then cut through the Lanes. Brighton's famous Lanes, selling their famous wares. Cheap at half the price. He went up North Street and swung left into Western Road. The winos were kicking each other outside the public toilets. They passed the foot of Brunswick Place.

"You can drop me by the newsagent's," she said.

He didn't slow down. He definitely didn't slow down. But neither did he perceptibly speed up. He just kept going at the same steady rate. He drove in the same way that he drilled – in no great hurry, biding his time, in total control.

"Anywhere along here," she said.

She glanced at the floral clock as they whisked on into Hove proper. She didn't want to be difficult. She wasn't the type to make a scene. A fuss was something she would try to avoid.

"This'll do fine."

They steamed down Church Road.

"I don't mind walking back."

They hung a right just past the Town Hall, then sharp left into the unattended, half-empty, multi-storey car park on Norton Road.

The car eased up the ramp and he took a ticket. They carried on round and up and round and up until they were

126

on the top floor. He turned off the ignition, and switched off the CD, and they sat in silence.

Alone in a car park on a Sunday afternoon. A quiet moment of contemplation. Reginald and Bella. Dentist and patient. Driller and killer.

# CHAPTER FIFTEEN

Water was running down one of the walls. It might have been a concrete wall. It might have been breeze-block. Or it might have been brick with something smeared on top. She doesn't know such things. She wished she did.

She wished she could watch the water run down the wall, and collect in a puddle on the floor, and know for sure what the wall was made of. It would have been reassuring to know. It would have given her a sense of certainty in an uncertain world. She likes certainties. She's a great believer in certainties. She hasn't got many, but she likes the ones she has.

She stared at the concrete stairway.

"Nice view," he said.

"Isn't it just."

"Makes a change to go somewhere different," he said.

"It certainly does."

A grin cracked open his face. He wore a set of superbly capped teeth, a gold signet-ring and ivory cufflinks. He was a jewelled man, who glittered and shimmered. A manicured man, with a well-trained wifey.

"Do you like my car?"

"I love your car."

"I love it too."

128

"I know you do."

"Do you think it's *me*?"

"Do I think it's you?" She considered for a moment. "I think it's more *me*."

"I've worked for this car."

"I'm sure you have."

"I've earned this car."

"And now it's yours."

Tiny bubbles appeared at the corners of his mouth when he spoke. He wasn't exactly frothing. It wasn't exactly gross. He just bubbled slightly when he spoke.

"I've worked hard to get the things I've got," he said. "I've worked damn bloody hard to get them, and I work damn bloody harder to keep them."

She emitted a sympathetic murmur. When the professional classes start to whinge, there's not a lot you can say. Maybe that's why he's brought her here. Maybe he just wants her to listen while he talks. Some men are like that. They take you to the top floor of an empty car park so they won't be disturbed while they talk.

"You wouldn't believe how bloody hard I bloody work."

He gripped the leather steering-wheel with his dental surgeon's hands.

"I've spent my whole bloody life bloody working."

"And not many can say that," she said.

"Poking around in people's mouths. Breathing in their bad breath. Wiping away their saliva."

"Looking up their nostrils . . . "

"Looking up their nostrils."

"You must be very proud, Reginald."

"Proud?! Why should I be proud? I get the dregs of the NHS. The absolute dregs. They foul up the waiting room and drop ash on the carpet and leer at Nursey with their rotting teeth and gum disease . . . "

"Patients require patience," she soothed.

" . . . and I lay on my hands, I bless them, I send them away whole again."

129

Dentistry and humility, she has often noticed, make uneasy companions.

"It's your vocation, Reginald," she reminded him. "Many are called, few are chosen."

He seemed to explode in his seat.

"But I've had enough, for Christ's sake! Can't you understand? Are you dense?"

He put his hand on her still-sore jaw and turned her face towards him. He pushed out her lips with his thumb and forefinger.

"My patients repel me. Do I make myself clear? I find them repulsive. I have to get inside their germ-filled mouths. I have to crawl inside their cavities and scrape out the decay."

"Someone's got to do it," she mumbled, through her pouted lips.

"But why *me*?"

"But why *not*?"

He shoved her head away.

"Because it's disgusting, that's why."

He flicked off the side-lights.

"I am a cultivated man. I have standards. I like things to be clean. I like clean things. I like clean people. I thought you'd understand."

"I think I'm beginning to."

"My wife understands. People should only try and understand. There's not enough understanding. I brought you here because I want you to understand."

She put another black mark against his name in her little red book. Two endorsements for Reggie. One more to go. Should she tell him? Should she warn him? Should she let him know it'll be curtains if he's not careful?

She decided against. She'd surprise him. A Bella surprise. She'd dish him out a Bella special. She's not too worried. She can handle it. She's calm. She's cool. She's collected. Two of them gone in twenty-four hours. Sent down to the cells. Two nosepickers gone. Two toerags removed. She'd kneecapped their brains. She'd done it herself, so she's not too concerned.

She might be a nobody, but the gun makes her somebody. She smiled a smug smile. With the gun in her bag, she can go where she likes. With the gun in her bag, he can rant and rave. With the gun in her bag, she can bide her time. With the gun in her bag . . . The smile froze on her face. There's no gun in her bag. The gun's by the bed.

"They've got odours. I can't bear their odours."

His North London voice was beginning to rasp.

"They try and cover it up with perfumes. They splash on scent and think I won't notice. Silly, smelly bitches. I can always tell. I bend over them and I smell their smell and sometimes I want to heave, I really want to heave."

"What smell?"

"That woman smell they've got. That smell you've all got. It clings to them, that stinking woman smell."

There's no gun in her bag.

"I smell it while I'm drilling their teeth. Vaginal discharge smell. Menstruation smell."

The gun's by the bed.

"I drill their teeth and I think of that muck that's oozing out of them, the muck that's staining my chair, that filthy female muck."

He stopped speaking. She listened to his watch ticking.

"What about men smells, then?"

"What about them?" he said.

"Don't they bother you?"

"Why should they?"

"No reason."

"I hope you understand now," he said.

"I think I do."

She pictured herself flinging open the door and running to the stairs. Running in her high heels across the empty top floor of an empty car park. The sound of her heels tip-tapping on the concrete. That useless, hopeless sound of high heels when they think they can get away.

131

You must have heard that sound, that staccato, woman sound. Clicking past your window when midnight's been and gone. Such a nervy, fragile, female sound.

Do you wonder what she's doing, out alone so late? Do you wonder what she's doing out there, all alone out there, tapping her way home in the dark? Do you purse your lips and wonder why she couldn't find anyone to hurriedly take her home, and take her hurriedly when he's got her home? That sound she makes, with her thin, high heels. It's such a lonely sound. The solitary sound of the slag, who can't afford a cab.

She could have leaped out of the car. Just flung open the door and leaped out of the car. She could have tripped along the concrete and up to the stairs. She could have clicked her way away from the car. She could have danced past the lift and up the ramp. But he'd be behind her. Breathing behind her. His bigness behind her. Breaking her butterfly arms as he dragged her back to the car.

So she sat in her seat and waited. She sat and waited while he rambled. She sat and listened, just like she used to do.

He took out his wallet and handed her a photograph. It showed a schoolgirl in maroon uniform. The photograph was a colour photograph, taken with one of those fixed-lens cameras that don't let you focus properly. The girl was smiling fuzzily, shielding her eyes from the sun.

"Your daughter?"

"My lovely daughter," he corrected. "My little pearl. My princess."

If you could have seen them sitting there, if you could have looked through the windows and seen them sitting in the front seats of the midnight blue Mercedes, you wouldn't have felt unduly alarmed, unless you were alarmist by nature. There was nothing in the scene that would have worried you, nothing to make you pause and ponder. You would have looked through the window and seen a middle-aged man in half-moon glasses hand a picture of

132

his daughter to his lady-friend, his lady-companion, his lady-acquaintance.

You might have noticed that her face had a grey, prison tinge, while his was florid with good living. You might have seen his fish-mouth open and close, but you would have heard nothing, for the windows were shut. You might have thought it slightly strange, the way he held the photo so carefully by its sides, without touching the print, as if afraid of soiling a sacred image.

But there was nothing peculiar, as such. There was nothing so unusual you would have peered closer. It was like the photo, the way they sat there. It looked fine on the surface. It looked so normal on the surface. It looked so decent and pure and wholesome on the surface. But you've got to go under the surface to find out what's there. You've got to lift up the stone to see what's underneath. You've got to scrape off the scab to examine the wound. You couldn't have guessed, from the way they looked, that he was burning and she was churning.

The bile was churning about in her belly. She could taste it in her mouth, together with bits of filling that she hadn't spat out. It was that fear taste, that terror taste that she used to taste from time to time. She'd let him get too close, and you can't let them get too close. Not if you're Bella. If you're Bella, you've got to keep your distance. Mustn't get too intimate, if you're Bella.

You can't let them get so close they can reach across and slap you with the flat of their open hand. A hard, controlled slap on your mouth, where Norman made you tender, so that your head would have snapped back but for the headrest.

He had that anxious, eager look they get when they've just struck a woman, and they know they'll strike her again. He had that look they get when they see a woman's head jerk back. The look of a man who knows he can shut her up. He can stop up her mouth. He can make her whimper at the sight of him. Such a heady feeling he had. Such a life-affirming, cloud-soaring, heady feeling when he slapped her hard on her mouth and her head jerked back.

"You weren't listening," he said. "If you don't listen, you won't learn."

He frowned.

"It's rude not to listen."

She put a hand to her mouth. Her lip had opened again. The way they kept splitting her lip open, she'd have to have it sewn up. She'd have to let someone insert needle and thread into her open lip and sew the sides together again.

Her mouth felt sore and broken, but her brain was cold and clear. It was a special kind of brain. It didn't bother with things that didn't interest it. The boredom threshold of Bella's brain, like its pain threshold, was unusually low. Most of the time it worked sluggishly, if it worked at all. But *in extremis*, at times of crisis, when the chips were down and the game was up and all seemed irretrievably lost, her brain would swell inside her head and press against her skull. It would sift and store and start to pulse.

And now it shuddered into gear. It juddered into action. It looked at them sitting there, in their leather seats, and it gave it to her straight, because her brain was a clear-sighted brain.

You've got no chance, it said. Silly girly, you'll have to give him what he wants. I would have told you, if you'd asked me.

You've swum out too far, you've toppled off your high-wire, your brakes have failed, your luck's run out. Brighton Bella. Boadicea Bella. All illusory.

You're in for it, now. I wouldn't want to be in your shoes. You'll get your comeuppance, that's what you'll get. Never take lifts. Never, ever take lifts. I've told you, often enough. But you got too cocky. You forgot that you're nothing without your weapons. Less than nothing. Minus nothing. And you left your weapons behind. You left them behind in the flat, you little fart.

134

I can't help you now. You can't talk your way out of this one. Silly billy Bella, I told you, but you wouldn't listen. You've always been wilful, and now you'll have to . . .

"Penny for them."

"What?"

"You looked miles away. Daydreaming. You want to concentrate a bit more on what people are saying to you."

"Sorry."

"Otherwise people might think you find them boring," he said. "I'm not boring you, am I?"

"Not at all," she said. "Not in the slightest."

"Because if I'm boring you, you must let me know, you really must."

"You're not," she said. "Really."

"About my daughter," he continued. "As I was saying."

She's all ears. He's hit her on the mouth, and she's all ears. Paying close attention. Straining hard. That's what you do when you're sitting in a car and the driver hits you on the mouth. If you're all alone, and he's opened your lip, and the gun's by your bed, that's what you do. You listen very hard to what he wants to say.

"My lovely daughter, who is the image of her lovely mother. I'm a doting father. A truly doting father. I dote on her. I suppose I'm a fool to myself, the things I buy that girl. You should see her bedroom. You should just see it. Everything pink and frilly. I wouldn't deny her anything. She's a lovely girl."

"A very lovely girl."

"A gorgeous girl. A really gorgeous girl. And very clean."

"You're very lucky."

"I know I am."

"She must be a great comfort to you."

"She is, she is. A very great comfort. She'd do anything for her Daddy."

"I'm sure she would."

"But I worry, too. She's at that age when you can't help worrying. Fourteen next spring."

135

His aftershave made her think of surfboards sliding over foam.

"Pubescent," he said, like it was some disease. "Maturing fast. She's maturing very fast. Developing, you might say. Becoming quite the little nubile."

He snatched the photo out of Bella's hand and stuffed it back in the wallet.

"Boys'll be coming round soon. Poking round. Sniffing round. It's sick."

"What's sick?"

"What men do to women. What women have done to them. I've read about it. The way they force women. It makes my blood boil. I can't understand it. It's just beyond me, the things they do."

He extended a hand and rested it lightly on her arm.

"You're too vulnerable. You're all too vulnerable, and I can't bear it. I want to protect you all. I don't know how you can bear to be so vulnerable."

"We try to manage as best we can."

"It must be dreadful being a woman," he said.

"It has its drawbacks."

"It can't be nice being a nice woman."

"I get by."

"I don't mean you," he said. "I don't think you're a nice woman."

The gun's by the bed. The gun's on a chair by the bed.

"Nice women," he said. "I like nice women."

His knuckles showed white on the steering-wheel.

"The thing about women," he said, "the thing about women that gets up my nose, is you never know what they're thinking, you never really know what they really want. Do you know what I mean?"

"Not really."

"I mean they doll themselves up, they tart themselves up, they let it all hang out, they act like they've been giving it away all their lives, they come on like all they want is a good hard screw and then you only have to look at them and

136

they start bleating, they start whining, I hate that woman's whine, that protracted female whine."

"I think it's time I had my tea."

"I mean they stick their smelly cunts in your face and what are you meant to do, what are you really meant to do?"

She watched the damp patch on the concrete.

"Answer me that," he said.

"Look," she said. "Reggie," she said.

"What I don't understand," he said, "what I really don't understand," he said, "is why you got into my car. What kind of girl gets into a man's car?"

"My kind."

"My daughter wouldn't get into a man's car. I've told her about men. I've taught her about men. She knows all about men. She knows not to sit in any man's car but my car. I've explained it all to her."

"That was very fatherly of you."

"She's only thirteen, but she knows what she'll get if she sits in someone's car. So if she knows it, you must know it. And if you know it, and you still came into my car, you must want it. And as you want it, you're going to get it."

"You offered me a lift," she said. "To Brunswick. A five-minute ride."

"A five-minute ride is what I offered, and a five-minute ride is what you'll get."

He reached across her and opened the glove compartment. A light came on inside and she saw two rolls of sticky tape and a pair of embroidery scissors and some green flex.

"It's not right," he said, taking out the flex and running it between his fingers. "It's not right, what you make us do."

"You don't have to do it. You don't have to, if you don't want to."

"But I do want to," he said. "I want to hugely. I want to immensely."

137

He took both her slim wrists in his left hand, and wound the flex around them with his right.

"I'm going to teach my daughter not to take risks," he said. "Why should she suffer because of sows like you?"

"You'll regret it, Reggie. You'll regret it later."

A flash of well-capped smile.

"Not as much as you will."

He pulled her forward across the gearshift and tied her wrists to the top of the steering wheel.

"You ought to floss your teeth. Night and morning. Brush and floss. Rub-a-dub scrub. Scrub away the stains. Early to bed and early to rise. Eat plenty of raw carrots, that's what I always say."

He removed an ultrabright linen handkerchief from his breast pocket. He parted his thighs and placed it on the seat.

"Cleanliness is next to godliness," he murmured.

He put his left hand behind her neck and held her tight. Had she been the type whose neck has a scruff, that would be where he gripped her.

"I hope you're hungry," he said, unzipping his fly, "because it's time for din-dins."

And he pushed her head down towards his thick and stubby cock.

"Open wide," he cooed.

# CHAPTER SIXTEEN

And Bella, in the instant when she's poised above him, her life flashing before her, sees the copper-coloured hairs, and smells that unwashed-penis smell, and reflects that this is something else her mother forgot to mention.

And then he's in her, and she's gagging, and he's holding her head with both hands and pushing her down and thrusting from the pelvis and he's filling her, stuffing her, choking her, and if her teeth were only sharper she'd clamp her jaws together like the Russian girl did to the German soldier.

It took a long time and a lot of friction before he was able to pump himself dry.

He groaned and relaxed and pulled her away by the hair.

"Have you swallowed?"

She was going to puke. She knew she was going to puke. He saw it on her face and quickly untied her and opened the door and stepped out.

"Got to have a slash," he said. "Have a good rinse."

She heard him walk over to the corner. She leaned over and spewed on to the concrete. She spewed out his taste and his stink and his slime. She kept on spewing until no more solids came up, only pale, sour stomach acids. Her face was burning with shame. She lifted her head and

139

watched him urinate against the wall of the lift. He was humming softly to himself.

Is this the end of Bella the brave, the dragon-slayer? Has she no choice but to slink back to her hole in the ground, her voice silenced, her mouth sticky with some degenerate's discharge? Must she crawl back to her lair, there to lick her wounds before shoving herself into a plastic bin-bag?

Is this it, then?

She looked at the keys in the ignition.

Perhaps not.

She eased herself over into the driver's seat, keeping her head below the sill. He had his broad back to her, as if she hadn't already seen all there was to see. He kept on pissing like he had a bottomless bladder. He'd been lugging around a full pack. No wonder he'd been irritable. Her head felt like it was cracking open.

Bastard prick. Son of prick.

Her fingers found the ignition. She sat up in the seat. A deep breath and she turned the key. The engine fired and he half-twisted, holding a flaccid penis in his hand.

Scum-faced dog. Piece of filth. Rot in hell.

All things come to she who waits. What was it Nimrod said? "Have patience, and the body of your enemy will be carried past your door." Nimrod knew a thing or two. But she had no patience. She couldn't wait for them to carry Reggie past. She couldn't leave him pissing in the wind. She couldn't leave him standing, after what he'd done.

She put the shift into Drive and slammed her foot down on the throttle. The Merc knifed forward. Two hundred horsepower in six cylinders knifed forward, and he was already moving aside when she smashed his left leg against the lift.

You should have heard him scream. Such a full-throated, uninhibited scream. A scream of pain and rage and fury, that would have curdled your blood if you weren't behind the wheel of a two-ton car.

The jolt of bumper against lift door sent her into the steering column, and she gasped from the sharp stab inside her chest. Putting the car into reverse, she sent it shrieking back, then slammed on the brakes. She flicked on the headlights, main beam. He was crawling around in a circle, screaming and sobbing and retching.

"I'll kill you, you bitch! You fucking crazy bitch!"

Big words. She laughed at the bigness of the big words.

He heaved himself to his feet and a spasm shook him and he staggered and nearly fell, and then he was standing again, and coming for her. Yes, he was coming for her. Here was a man who couldn't recognise reality, even when it smashed his left leg against a lift door.

She reversed five yards and braked. He stopped moving and stared at her. She gunned the engine. He looked like a rabbit in the beams. She released the brake and put her foot down on the throttle. She put her foot down hard on the throttle, and she thrust forward, she surged forward, she powered forward.

This time it was a full frontal collision. A head-on smash between Reggie and Reggie's car. The car he'd bloody worked so bloody hard for crushed into him. Bloodily. The impact was so harsh that he jack-knifed on to the hood, and banged over the roof, and slithered down the other side.

And this is what it feels like to commit Reggicide: You move the car back, and it goes over something soft, like a rubber hump in the road, but you don't really feel it because the suspension's so good. And you go forward again. And back again. And forward again. And each time the hump feels slightly different. Slightly lower. Slightly softer.

And you do this a few times. Repeatedly. Relentlessly. And you wish you could see what you're doing. You'd really rather see what you're doing. So you take it further back and dip the lights. And there's Reggie. Reggie the veggie. With his legs at odd angles and the tiniest red trickle seeping from the corner of his lips.

Her mouth felt foul. The dirty beast had dirtied her, so she'd wiped away the stain. He knew the rules, anyway. He behaved unprofessionally, so she struck him off.

She stared at what was left of him. She'd have to leave him there. He was too heavy to lift. If she could have lifted him, she would have tucked him into the trunk. She would have levered him into that sporty little trunk, before rigor mortis stiffened the mush she'd made of him. Reggie would have got the order of the trunk. But, alas and alack, it was not to be. He was too strong for her, even now. She checked her hair in the vanity mirror. Dishevelled, she was. There was no other word for it. She wondered how some women always managed to look so well-groomed.

She drove out of the car park. He wouldn't be found till the next day. Nobody came there on a Sunday. Decent people didn't go to empty car parks on a Sunday. Only creeps and pervs. Low-life. Scumbags. And they'd read about it. They'd read all about it in their local freesheet. They'd hear about it on the radio. They'd watch a reconstruction on the box.

And when they heard the phrase, "evidence of recent sexual activity", they'd know that the walls were closing in on them, their freedoms were being chipped away, the worms were very definitely turning.

She drove out on to the street. The car-clock read ten past six. It was dark on the street. *Le tout* Hove seemed to be indoors for the duration. She drove back to Brunswick, and went round her block. As she passed Timothy's building, she looked for the thin blue line, but it was nowhere in sight. There was no white tape across the pavement. No incident vehicle. No stiffnecked probationer standing guard outside. No sweat.

Back to her own flat. Her own, shortly to be abandoned, unlikely to be missed, flat. The source of her damnation and her salvation. Her nest, her rented rat-hole, her little box of tricks.

She felt tired. She wanted to sleep. She wanted to lie

142

down and forget and let sleep drift into her. But she knew she couldn't. Not yet. She had to move fast, now. She'd been lucky, so far. But no-one's that lucky for that long. You can't push it too much. You've got to make your break some time. You've got to call it a day, some time. You can't go on forever. Not even a Bella can go on forever.

She packed a bag with toiletries and shoes, then crammed clothes on top. She counted out the money she had left. Less than two hundred. Not much. Not much to start a new life. She should have robbed Reginald. She should have lifted the wallet off that dental defective. But it hadn't occurred to her, in the excitement of the moment. You can't think of everything. She brewed up some tea, and nibbled a digestive, and pondered her future.

It would have to be London. London was the place for her. You could lose yourself in London. You lose yourself, and then you find yourself. Brighton was too provincial, anyway. Too parochial. Too much the seedy little seaside town, where nothing ever happened. She would go to London and find a flat, and find a job, and find a man. A gentle kind of man, who wouldn't give her pain.

She'd go tomorrow. You shouldn't rush these things. She'd slope up to the big city tomorrow. She went into the bedroom and picked up the gun. It had cost her four hundred pounds. The clip contained six bullets. Nearly seventy pounds a bullet. She'd use it tonight. Use it and chuck it away. She'd pull the trigger six times. She'd fire it six times. She'd feel it buck six times.

She slipped it into her handbag, hooked the bag over her shoulder, and picked up the small suitcase. She turned off the gas and electricity and covered the bed and checked all the locks. When all was done, she stepped out into the patio and pulled the door shut behind her.

Up the steps and into the road. Her car was gleaming. A gleaming car. Definitely more her than him, that car. She put her suitcase and handbag on the passenger seat, and walked round and climbed inside. She hadn't thrown

143

anything away. She hadn't disposed of anything that would identify her. She wanted to make things easy for them, when they came.

She took her foot off the brake and the midnight-blue Mercedes pulled away from the curb.

They'd come tomorrow, or the next day. They'd come and they'd see and they'd know who she was. Let them know. She wanted them to know. She wanted them to know her name.

# CHAPTER SEVENTEEN

At half-past ten that night, as she sliced into a fairly thick steak in a fairly French restaurant, three men were walking down Cheapside.

Across town, near the station, where you wouldn't want to lurk if you could help it, three young men were walking down Cheapside. They came together and fell apart as they walked, laughing and joking and barely touching.

One was small. One was quiet. And one was bitter.

They dressed like lords and they spoke like plebs. They loathed what they couldn't understand. They shared each other's tastes, and shared each other's women, and loved each other, the way men do. The jackets they wore were Armani jackets. Real Armani jackets. Gospel Armani, not off-the-peg Armani. They liked to get their jackets dirty, of an evening. It reminded them how rich they were. They liked to get their jackets ripped in a midnight ruck, then chuck them away and buy another.

They weren't exactly looking for trouble, although they welcomed it when they found it. It helped them relax, after spinning fortunes in the City, to come back to Brighton and bait a few yokels on the pier. In Brighton they swam with the big fish. They went drinking with antique dealers, and to the races with property rats. They could really enjoy having money in Brighton. They just had to look at the jerks who had none. They liked to drive around, on weekday nights. They'd cruise around in their cars and slow down near some bus-stop and gob in the face of a local lad. High-spirited they called it, though you might have called it uncalled-for.

Gobbing was one of their pastimes. When they weren't buying options, or selling futures, they were gobbing. They had gobbing contests on the Tube, in tight-packed trains, where people couldn't move. They hawked up phlegm and spat it at the ceiling handgrips that wobbled on the bends.

You had to laugh.

The man who took their tickets at Victoria Station called them lager louts. The bitter one head-butted him. We're not lager louts, he said, as they watched him crumple in his kiosk. We're champagne shits.

They were too fit. They shouldn't be so fit, the jobs they do. They worked out at City gyms. Maybe that was the secret. But they didn't live there. Docklands couldn't keep them. They'd each bought Regency houses on Brighton's more elegant crescents. They could live well in Brighton. They had a good life in Brighton. They had style, they had money and they had arrived.

Some people have so much they seem to shimmer as they walk. They glitter with good fortune, and you want to kiss their hem in gratitude when their shadow flits across your face. They've got a kind of sun-bleached beauty they let you see but not touch. It must frighten them, sometimes, to be so young and to have so much.

They were like that, these three, wandering through Cheapside in their designer jackets. They had everything, and they knew they had everything, and it seemed only right that they had everything.

Why they went down that particular dark alley, we'll never know. It was blocked off at the end, so there was one way in, and one way out. It was what is known as a blind alley.

You really shouldn't venture down a blind alley, if you

146

can possibly avoid it. Even if there's three of you, and your voices carry through the night, you shouldn't go down a blind alley. You shouldn't step from a main road into a side road, and from the side road into a black hole that leads nowhere.

It's not illegal, but it's not advisable.

Bella wouldn't have done it. The old Bella, who became the shed skin of the new Bella, wouldn't have done it. The blithe rashness of the act was something she just wouldn't have done.

But you can't expect young men, with voices like those voices, to feel like a Bella. You can't expect them to tread softly, like a Bella. You can't expect them to hesitate, when every building, every patch of grass, every dim-lit street, every station, every subway, every blind alley belongs to them, and they can enter if they wish. You can't expect them to feel like a Bella, who felt like a trespasser in her own home.

They went into the alley, the three of them, and their voices ran on ahead. Their voices buffeted the windowless walls that looked down blindly into the blind alley. The sound of their steps, as they stepped in deeper, was such a confident sound. They stepped onward and inward into the narrow alley, laughing and braying and whistling in the dark.

The light from the streetlamp that shone from the road got fainter and fainter, so that it barely touched the heap of charity clothes that shook and shivered at the far end.

She could have been sixty, or fifty, or seventy. It's hard to tell when they get like that. She wore three jumpers and two coats and woollen gloves with the fingers cut off, and every so often she scratched her scalp. She sat by herself at the end of the alley. She pointed a bony finger and counted them: One, two, three, she said, lisping through her bottom dentures. Her mouth seemed to have collapsed in on itself.

They stood in a semicircle around her. Their faces were black against the dim orange light seeping in from the street.

147

Sharp clouds of frost formed halos above their heads. She thought they looked like angels.

The small one spoke first.

"What have we here?"

The quiet one said nothing.

The small one glanced at the bitter one.

"Is it human?"

"A piece of scrag," the bitter one said. "A scraggy old bag."

The small one shook his head sadly.

The quiet one grinned at the brick wall behind her.

She sat and shivered on the ground. They seemed to be growing. The longer she looked at them the bigger they grew. They grew as they gazed at the end of the alley. She shouldn't have wandered off. She was always wandering off. She needed a drink. She'd only had cider all evening, and she needed a drink, and she knew she shouldn't have wandered off.

"What's your name?"

Her eyes slid across to the small one. He had a very deep voice for such a small man. He spoke very slowly and very clearly. The small ones were always the worst ones.

"Mary," she said.

"Mary what?"

"Liverpool Mary."

There were two carrier bags on either side of her. A canvas holdall lay in her lap, and she wrapped her arms around it.

"That's a pity, Mary," the small one said, touching one of the plastic bags with the tip of his boot, "because we don't like scousers down here."

"Dirty people, Mary."

"Thieves."

"Paddies."

"Parasites."

"Spitting on our pavements."

"Shitting in our gardens."

148

"We don't like them, Mary."

"We hate them, Mary."

The bitter one bent down and grabbed the holdall from her lap.

"It's an offence to litter the street."

He drew back the zip and peered inside.

"It's against the bye-laws."

He upended the bag and tipped out the contents.

"Welcome to Brighton."

The small one laughed. Mary was glad she'd made someone laugh. She smiled gummily into the dark.

"I think she's backward," the bitter one said.

"A retard," the small one agreed.

"I had a mongol, once."

"Did she like it?"

"She didn't say."

The small one lit a cigarillo with a gold-plated lighter. He held the flame close to her face. Her eyes were opaque. She had opaque, unfocused, milky eyes. A scrap of green ribbon was tied in her hair.

"Do you want her?"

"My dog wouldn't want her."

The bitter one looked at her bitterly. She was an ugly woman, and he detested ugly women.

"She smells," he said.

The small one nodded.

"She stinks."

The quiet one opened his mouth.

"She positively reeks."

The bitter one pressed the sole of his shoe against the side of her face, and pushed her face into the damp brick wall. They laughed when he did that. You had to laugh, she looked so funny. Her cheeks ballooned out between his shoe and the wall.

"Pig-face," the small one said.

You really had to laugh. Even the bitter one had to laugh. He took his foot away from her face and scraped his shoe on the ground, as if he'd stepped in something nasty. He didn't yet know what he would do to her, but he knew he would do something.

"I think," he said, "we should take her walkies."

He reached down and gripped her oldwoman hair. He was such a strong young man. It's not as if he pulled so hard. It shows how decayed she was, what a living, rotting corpse he had at his feet, that a handful of hair came out of the shiny scalp. The quiet one, who had a delicate stomach, looked quietly away.

She gazed up at the bitter one with her milky eyes. A small sound came from her mouth.

"Did you say something?" he said. "I believe you said something."

He glanced at the small one, then back at the woman.

"I think she swore at me."

The top of her head was bleeding, though you couldn't see it clearly in the dark.

"Did she swear at me?" the bitter one asked the quiet one.

The quiet one didn't answer.

"She did," the small one said.

The bitter one shook his head.

"A foul-mouthed woman."

The small one nodded.

"Not a lady."

"A woman who's not a lady," said the bitter one, "is a degradation to her sex."

The small one puffed cigar smoke into the night air. "A woman who's not a lady," he said, "needs lessons in etiquette."

The bitter one bent down and whispered in her ear.

"We're going to give you some lessons," he said. "Back to school we go."

He liked the way she shrank from him. He liked the way her fingers gripped at nothing and her concave mouth trembled in her face. He liked the way she cringed, but he hated her for cringing.

150

"She's got to be taught."

"If she's not taught, she won't learn."

"She needs a short sharp shock."

"Or a long fat cock."

"Do you fancy me, grandma?"

She shook her head.

"I think she's got someone."

"One of the Norfolk Square scumbags."

"Is that right, granny? Are you making it with a wino?"

Spittle spilled out of her slack jaw.

"I think we should take a look at granny's fanny."

They glanced at each other.

"Cut through the cobwebs."

"The dust of ages."

"Have a general poke around."

"Find out what's what."

"Please . . . "

"Did she say something rude again?"

"She did."

"She's going to be difficult."

"She's going to be troublesome."

"Mary, Mary, quite contrary."

"Please don't . . . "

"Don't what?" the bitter one asked. "We can do what we like. We're the police." He smiled at his friends. "We're the law."

He punched her on the side of the head.

"And that was our strong arm."

The wail that came out of her filled up the alley. It rose and fell. It dipped and swayed like a reed in the wind. Mummmeeeeeeeeeee! A strange and animal sound. They shivered when they heard it.

The quiet one sniggered.

The small one flicked ash from the end of his cigar.

The bitter one pulled her up by her elbows. He clamped a hand over the open mouth.

"She wants her mater."

151

She was just bones. Skin and bones and bad smells. He didn't know how people could get like that. They deserved all they got, if they got like that. He released his grip and let her drop.

The quiet one stared at his shoes as she collapsed like an empty sack. The small one bent and sat her up again.

"We only want to examine you," he said. "We want to make sure you've got all your bits."

The bitter one nodded.

"We want to make sure you haven't got nits."

"It's for the best," the small one said. He put his arm around her shoulder. "You'll thank us for this one day."

"You'll like it, Mary," the bitter one added. He stuck his hands in his pockets and grinned at his friends. "You really will."

She was wearing several layers of clothing. Her clothing was multi-layered. She'd been wearing the layered look for years. They took off all her layers and left her in her underwear. The bitter one watched as she shook in the alley. There was no shape to her. She was shapeless. A shapeless lump. A bow-legged, arthritic, shapeless lump.

"The vest," he said.

The quiet one mumbled something.

The bitter one turned to the quiet one.

"If you want us to stop, we'll stop."

The quiet one shrugged.

"You want us to stop?"

The quiet one looked at the bitter one. The small one smiled at the quiet one.

"We'll stop if you want. You want us to stop?"

The quiet one stared at the old one.

"Don't stop," he said.

The small one pulled the vest over her head. She began to cry. They stared at the breasts that hung down to her waist. Her dried-out, dangling, oldwoman breasts. They had to laugh. They couldn't help it. They had to laugh.

152

She stood in her pants, with her bleeding scalp, and cried as they laughed in a blocked-off alley.

"Touch her," the bitter one said.

"You touch her."

He put out a hand and touched the crepey skin of her stomach. It puckered beneath his fingers. Paper-thin skin that made him sick. He flicked a breast with his thumb.

"She's got warts," he said.

His head was bursting. He couldn't bear the sight of her. The smell of her was worse than the sight of her. The feel of her was worse than the smell of her. She made his head begin to burst. She made him wild. The clapped-out whining crone, she made him wild. She shouldn't have sat at the end of the alley. She shouldn't have let him find her. She shouldn't have been so helpless. She shouldn't have been at all.

"Witches have warts," the small one said.

The bitter one held her by the elbows. She weighed nothing at all. He put his face close to hers.

"Do you know something, Mary?" He ran a finger under her chin. "You're growing a beard."

"You're not taking care of yourself."

"You're letting yourself go."

"Every night, Mary," the bitter one said, "every night you've got to cleanse, tone and moisturise."

"If you want soft skin."

"Skin that's smooth to touch."

"Supple skin."

The scalp that wasn't torn glimmered through the tufts that remained. She blinked at them. It's not new to her, what's happening. Not a total novelty. Not unprecedented. Sometimes she has quiet nights, and sometimes she doesn't. She's been there before. She's had things done to her before. She shouldn't have wandered off. They wouldn't have found her, if she hadn't wandered off.

"I think," the bitter one said, "that what we have here is an environmental problem."

He held her tight. She was better off dead.

"I think," he said, "we should Keep Britain Tidy."

He clamped a hand on her chin. Saliva trickled over his fingers. He wanted them to stop him. He wanted them to pull him away and make him stop. It wasn't his fault. He knew it wasn't his fault. If it was anyone's fault, it was probably hers.

"What are we going to do?" the quiet one asked.

The bitter one felt her tremble. It made him hard, the way she trembled. What should they do with her? What shouldn't they do with her? He had to do something. He had to do something soon. He had to do something soon to get rid of the stench.

"Let's burn her."

The small one sucked in his breath.

The quiet one went very quiet.

"Let's burn the witch," the bitter one said.

He had his hand on her throat. He could have squeezed her windpipe and felt it snap. Her frailty revolted him. He hated her more completely than he'd ever hated anyone.

Sometimes you think certain thoughts, but you don't say them. They're such dirty thoughts that you can't believe you can even think them. You think no-one else could possibly think those thoughts, so you keep them to yourself. You keep your dirty thoughts piled up inside your head in a little heap of thoughtful dung.

But one night, one cold, clear February night, with your hand on her throat and your brain on a high, you pluck one of those thoughts from the pile. You speak your unspoken thought, and it doesn't seem so dirty when you say it out loud. Let's burn her, you say. The words sound all right at the back of an alley.

Let's burn her, you think, and you say it out loud. And once you've said it, you've got to do it. Let's burn her. It doesn't seem so dirty when you say it. There's almost something clean about it, when you really think about it.

The small one and the quiet one and the bitter one

stared at each other. Then they stared at her. They were out for a laugh. No harm meant. No offence intended. They only wanted to watch her burn. They wanted to test her flammability factor. They wanted to hear her sizzle where she sat. They wanted to roast her like a rissole. She was a dosser, so she was going to burn. It happens, now and then.

The bitter one had a pink paper, which he tore into uneven strips.

"No *FT*, no comment."

He stuffed bits of polished prose into her mouth, and under her arms, and behind her ears. He shredded the unit trust columns into her hair. He scrunched up the editorial and dropped it in her lap. He put wads of situations vacant into her cupped hands. He fetched the cardboard box she would have slept in, and slit it up its sides, and placed the damp squares around her, like a little pyre.

"You look grand," he said. "You'll get your name in the papers," he said. "And that can't be bad."

The other two watched him work. They thought it made a difference, if they only watched. They wanted him to light the fuse, to bomb her into oblivion. They wanted him to stop and save her. They wanted to run out of the alley, but not until they'd watched her blacken. They wanted him to do it for them, to light the match and fling it at her feet. She didn't matter, anyway. An unproductive element, whose pain would give them pleasure.

The small one emptied the contents of his hip-flask over her head. She put out her tongue and licked around her lips.

"Ashes to ashes, dust to dust," the quiet one said.

"Bring on the barbecue," the bitter one said.

He felt so good. He felt rock-hard, and it felt so good. He unbuttoned his fly.

"Look at this," he said. "Have a good look," he said. "Have a last good look."

She shut her eyes and rocked herself from side to side. Bits of newsprint fell to the ground.

155

You had to laugh.

The quiet one handed the bitter one a box of matches. The small one took them from him.

"Let me do it," he said. "I want to do it."

The bitter one smiled at the small one. He loved him like a brother. The quiet one saw the smile and wanted to share it.

The old one also saw the smile. She saw the matches in the small one's hand. She saw the shining sun devour him. A blinding light came beaming on her face.

They saw her white and semi-naked with bits of paper in her mouth. They heard a soft and throaty growl come crawling up the alleyway. They turned and watched as two bright eyes came creeping up the alleyway. Metal glinted in the orange light. The streetlamp threw stars on a polished roof. The shape became a two-seat coupé. It drove right down the middle, with inches clear on either side.

That's the thing about a Merc. It purrs up on people. It purrs up behind them. It's a very devious car.

It stopped about four yards back. The well-oiled engine barely murmured. They couldn't see the driver. The windscreen was pitch black behind halogen headlights. They listened to the continental engine. Mary sat behind them. She sat against the wall, her breasts on her belly and listened to the murmur of a German-made engine.

The halogens snapped off. They saw the driver's shape inside the car. They didn't want to move before they had to move. A vanity light came on. They saw a woman in the driver's seat. She pulled down a mirror and checked her hair. The silly bitch. The silly interfering bitch. They grinned at each other. They grinned at the driver. As long as she didn't back down the alley, they'd be all right. As long as she didn't go for help, they'd be okay. As long as she stepped out of the car, they were in the clear.

Four sets of eyes watched as the woman climbed out and hooked a heavy handbag over her shoulder. She left the engine running.

"Are you joining us?" the bitter one called.

"We're having a party," the small one added.

"The more the merrier."

Mary began to cry.

The woman with the handbag had left the car door open. She'd stepped out of the car, and left the door open behind her. The handbag-woman had blocked her own escape. If she had to run in a hurry, she'd have to get round the other side. And she wouldn't have time to get round the other side, if she had to get away in a hurry. They could all see it. It was clear for all to see, and they could all see it. Even Mary could see it, and when she saw it she began to cry.

# CHAPTER EIGHTEEN

The small one walked slowly towards the Mercedes.

"You shouldn't be out so late," he said.

"Why not?"

"You don't know who you'll meet."

She smiled in the dark.

"Neither do you."

He stopped about a yard away.

"I rather think you might have pissed off when you had the chance," he said.

"Do you rather?"

"I do."

She looked at him. He was a very small man. The smaller the man, the bigger the ego. She's often noticed that. Everyone's noticed that. It takes no talent to notice that. She doesn't dislike small men. Not particularly. Not especially. Not unless they think they'll have her. If they think they'll have her, if they get too big for their tiny boots, if they think they'll climb up on an orange box and have a Bella, it makes her rather squirm. The cheek of it. The self-deluding nerve of it.

It makes her want to squash them down. It makes her want to tread on them. To stamp on them. To smear them on the pavement. But apart from that, apart from what she wants to do if they want to have her, she doesn't mind them. She doesn't *like* them, but she doesn't mind them. They only mustn't think they'll have her. They mustn't think they'll get inside her. They mustn't walk towards her in an alley, with that small-man smirk upon their face.

She looked at him, the tiny man.

"What're you doing?"

"Visiting Grandma." A very deep voice, for such a very small man.

He was eyeing the car.

"Nice motor," he said. "Had it long?"

"Not very."

"Your bloke's car?"

"My car."

"You must be doing all right."

"I get by."

"What's your line, then?"

"Waste disposal."

"Mucky work, for a woman."

"Where there's muck there's brass."

"You don't mind getting your hands dirty?"

"A girl has to do what a girl has to do."

She saw the matches in his palm.

"What're you doing?"

She doesn't like having to repeat herself.

"We're having a private conversation," he said. "Like woman-talk," he said, "only it's man-talk. Not your thing, I would have thought."

"Don't mind me."

"I won't," he said.

He struck a match against the box. The flame flared blue. Wind snuffed it out. She liked the flame. It set her thinking. She's always liked the smell of burning. She likes the bonfires in the park. She's not averse to arson. Not as such.

But setting fire to living people, burning real and breathing people, making ash of broken people?

159

She watched him fumble with the matches.
"You shouldn't play with fire," she said.
"You're very talkative," he said.
"You play with fire and you might get burned."
"I think you think we're up to something."
"I think you're going to torch your granny."
The small one smiled and turned to his friends.
"She thinks we're horrid hooligans."
"That's a slanderous statement, I'd say," the bitter one said.
"And very hurtful," the quiet one added.
They came and stood next to the small one. They were three, in the alley. She was one. They measured her with their eyes. She looked brittle. She had a brittle look, when you really looked.
"Your penis is hanging out," she said to the bitter one.
"It's sticking out," he said.
"Time to put it away," she said. "Time to put away childish things."
He stepped closer.
"Have you ever been penetrated," he enquired politely, "from behind?"
She watched them watching her. They were three, in the alley, and she was one. Three strong young men. Three musketeers. Three brave young bloods. Three too many. Three lemmings. Three little lambs. Three martyrs to her cause.
She slid her hand inside the bag. Her fingers closed around the gun. She held it gently. She held the gun inside the bag. She warmed the metal with her touch. She held the gun, and looked at them, and felt her courage grow.
This is the moment. The moment of moments. Her finger touched the trigger. Her finger rested on the trigger. She had her finger on the trigger. Would it be too stiff for her? It wouldn't be. It couldn't be. Life might be cruel, but it has its consolations. And one of life's consolations is that a trigger's never too stiff.

"She's got an alarm," the small one said. "She's about to set off a stupid alarm."

"Nobody ever comes," the bitter one said. "Nobody cares. Nobody will even hear."

"I know," she said.

It was so deserted, round there. It was such a bleak, empty, deserted place, round there. Near the goods yard, behind the station, away from the bright lights of the seafront. You wouldn't want to loiter round there. You shouldn't go into an alley round there. Not when you never know who might come in behind you.

She had her hand in the bag and the gun in her hand. Fear no evil. Put your trust in the sword, and your sword in the foe. It was such a sweet moment. She wanted to prolong the moment. She wanted to savour the sweetness of the sweet moment.

"Bend over the hood," the bitter one said.

"Chop-chop," the quiet one said.

The small one ground the cigar beneath his heel.

"You're going to get three city slickers inside your knickers."

She looked up at the night sky. She didn't know you could feel so alive. She felt giddy with life. She wanted to tell them. She wanted to thank them. She wanted to bless them. She uttered a silent prayer: for what they were about to receive, let the Lord make her truly grateful.

What happened next was like the movies. It was cinematic in scope. It had definite filmic potential. The small one came up to her and put his hand on the strap of her bag. He was pulling it away from her, he was pulling the bag away from her so that he could push her down on the hood. She saw his hand on her shoulder-strap. She watched him move. She watched his movements. They were slow-motion movements, in a slow-motion movie. It was Pekinpah, without the dust.

He had his hand on the strap. He was pulling the bag off her shoulder. He had that small-man glee in his eyes. That

161

look of small-man triumph they get when they're about to prove that they're not so small, after all. He was going to have her. He was going to have her on the hood of her husband's car.

"Get in there, my son."

She looked into his face. There was a smile on his face. He had his hand on the strap. He had his smooth little hand on the strap of her bag. She looked into his face as he pulled at her strap. She looked into his face and she saw his smile and she felt the familiar burning.

She brought out the gun. She lifted the gun right out of the bag. She held the gun in her lilywhite hand. She pressed the gun right into his belly. She pressed it into his babysoft belly.

He felt her push right into his belly. He felt her try to push him away. She pressed what he thought was her bitch-hard finger into the flesh of his babysoft belly. He pulled the bag away from her shoulder. He let it slide and fall to the ground. He kept on smiling.

He'd have the bitch. He was going to have her. He'd have her first, before the others. He'd make her bend. He'd make her bend right over the hood. He'd bend her, then he'd bugger her. The stuck-up bitch. The stinking stuck-up bitch, who thought she was too good for him. By the time he'd finished, she'd know a bit better. She'd know that she wasn't too good for him. She'd know that she wasn't too good for anyone.

But she kept on pushing right into his belly. She was pushing her finger right into his belly. It felt like a rod, like a cold piece of pipe. He quickly glanced down, and he saw what it was that she'd pushed in his belly.

He might have said "oh". He might have said "ah". Whatever it was, it was lost in the wind. They were standing so close. Indecently close. Her finger on the trigger, and the barrel in his belly.

She gave the small one a second or two. A second or two, to let him look up. She let him look up and lock

162

eyes with her. They looked at each other, the small one, the still one. The knowing look that passed between them. The look of surprise at the way things turn out. Hunter become quarry. Quarry become hunter. Executioner condemned. Condemned – executioner. The knowingness of the look that passed between them.

She gave him a second, or two, or three, before she gave him eternal damnation. A moment or two to prepare himself. To gird up his loins. To straighten his back. To salvage his soul.

"Get on with it," the bitter one called. He couldn't have seen what she held in her hand.

"All right," she replied.

She squeezed the trigger. A gentle squeeze. She could barely miss. Not with it right there. Right there in his belly. They say that you always miss your first. But she didn't miss. He was her first, and she didn't miss.

Something warm splashed on to her and his arms came up and he seemed to bend towards her and then he jerked back and twisted and fell down on the ground.

She didn't hear the bang. There must have been a bang, but she never heard it. He had a dark stain on his shirt-front. If he'd worn a coloured shirt, it wouldn't have shown up as dark as it did. He was twitching as he lay on the ground. She'd seen a black cat knocked down once. A rather unlucky black cat. It had also twitched like that. The driver hadn't stopped.

The bitter one stared at the body on the ground. The quiet one stared at the gun. The bitter one began to back down the alley. He backed slowly down the alley, away from her, towards the old woman with newsprint in her hair. The quiet one didn't move.

She looked down at the small one. His eyes were wide open. Spasms shook his legs.

"Shall I put him out of his misery?" she asked the quiet one. She turned to face him.

"Shall I mercy-kill your colleague?"

163

The quiet one was shaking his head. He kept shaking his head. He didn't move, but he opened his mouth and he shook his head.

"It wasn't my idea. It's nothing to do with me. I wasn't going to do anything. They made me. I didn't want to. I took no part . . . "

She blew a large hole in the small one's head.

That time she heard the bang.

She turned back to the quiet one. He was shaking. He was shaking with fear, like she used to shake. Wide-eyed with terror. Bug-eyed with dread. She was getting aggravation from watching him shake.

"Don't hurt me," he said. Appealing, cajoling. The soft-spoken incendiarist asking for mercy. Pleading. Begging. "I'm not like them. It wasn't me. Don't shoot. Don't hurt me."

He pointed a finger at his bitter best friend.

"Shoot him, not me!"

He had his hand in front of him, as if a hand could shield him. He held his hand in front of him, the palm towards her, fingers spread apart.

"It wasn't me," he said again. "I'm on your side."

She took her time, this time. The aim was very true. She caught him in mid-scream, just below his not-very-prominent Adam's apple. He dropped to his knees. She would have thought he'd keel over, but he didn't. He just dropped to his knees. She stepped up close. He was in dire need of a tracheotomy.

"You can dish it out, but you can't take it," she said. "You're all give, and no take." She shot him in the chest, where his heart could well have been.

Four rounds gone. Two left. The engine was still running. Sweet as sugar, that engine was. They know how to build cars, the Krauts. You've got to give them that. They're great at building cars. But she still would have preferred a Jag. Buying British was one of her things.

She found, when she pulled the trigger, that she used a

single-handed action. She thought she'd have to use both hands, but it proved unnecessary. There was hardly any recoil, either. It only lifted, ever so slightly.

The bitter one was crouched beside the old one. She walked towards him. Traces of vomit showed on his chin. He was rubbing his knuckles against the ground. She stood in front of him, aiming down.

"And then there was one."

The old one had put her arm around the bitter one. She began to rock him to and fro. She pulled his head against her lips and kissed his downy cheek.

Bella pointed the gun at the space between his eyes.

"Get up," she said.

"Make me."

"Get away from her and get up."

"Eat shit."

He'd buttoned up his fly. He wasn't going to die with his fly wide open. He wasn't going to beg her, like the quiet one. Nor get it in the stomach, like the small one. He wanted to watch her when she did it. He was going to die, and he didn't want to die. He cursed his bad luck. He wasn't bitter for nothing.

"Do it," he said.

"I never shoot a man when he's down."

"Do it now," he said.

"Get up."

"Kill me now, you cunt."

"Granny says it's time to go."

He looked up at her. He grinned at her. He was a lovable rogue. Everyone thought so. A wicked angel. He grinned at her. He was a charmer. Everyone thought so.

Had there been a hammer on the pistol, she would have cocked it. It was the moment to cock the hammer. She should have got a revolver. A revolver would have been better. There's no hammer you can cock on an automatic pistol.

The old woman was caressing him, crooning into his

ear. She'd always wanted a baby of her own. He watched Bella take a few steps back. He didn't want to die. He looked into the unblinking black eye of the barrel and realised how deeply he didn't want to die.

"Get up," she said.

He smiled his roguish smile at her. It often worked.

"If you insist," he said.

He pushed away the old one and stood up. The yellow light fell on him at a different angle, and his eyes disappeared into black-hole sockets. He felt better once he was standing. He'd forgotten how much he liked to stand. He did his very favourite things – his pissing, screwing – always standing.

"I've got kids," he said. "Think of my kids."

"You think of them."

"You'll be killing their dad."

"You're too young for kids. Too young and too greedy and in too much of a hurry."

"I need a cigarette."

"So have a cigarette."

He slipped a hand inside his jacket and brought out a silver cigarette-case. He placed a filter-tip in his mouth.

"Got a light?"

She laughed noiselessly. A gutsy sort of bastard. He might have been a prick, but he had his pride. Shame she had to blow him away. Almost a shame.

"I never carry one."

"Let me go," he said. "I'll pay you if you let me go. I've got money." He fingered his lapel. "Loadsarmani."

"You've got it on you?"

"It's at home. I keep a lot of cash at home."

"I don't go to men's flats any more."

"I haven't got a flat. I've got a house."

"You mean you had a house. Like you had a life."

"We can go and get the money."

"What makes you think I want money?"

"Everyone wants money."

"You don't know what I want."

"What do you want?"

"I want you to shut your eyes and think of England."

"I don't want to die," he said. Obvious perhaps, but it needed saying.

"You should have thought of that before."

"Before what?"

"Before you walked down this alley."

"I wasn't to know you'd come in firing."

"She wasn't to know you'd come in burning."

"Fair point," he said, "fair point."

"I'm glad you think so."

"I'm glad you're glad," he said, and bellowed like a bull, and flung the silver ciggy box into her face, and leaped at her with flailing fists.

He wasn't stupid. He might have been bitter, but he wasn't stupid. He did what you're meant to do, when confronted with a gunperson. You throw something at them and follow through with a charge. It's a very commando-like thing to do. He had probably been in his school's Combined Cadet Force. It was his moment, and he seized it. He tried. He was a trier. You could see why he'd done well in the markets. As has been said, he bellowed as he lunged at her. You're meant to do that, too. It distracts the gunperson.

He only had to cross a few feet. A yard or two, perhaps. He only had to fling himself a corpse-length forward, and knock her gun-hand in the air. It wasn't a lot for him to do. But she only had to pull the trigger. Sometimes even not a lot can be too much.

He came at her, bellowing. He bellowed as he charged at Bella. She hadn't been in the CCF. She hadn't been schooled in martial arts. But you don't have to drill, to know how to kill. She was a natural. It came easily to her. It was breathing in fresh air. It was doing what you were meant to do. It was glorious.

So when he flung himself at her, when he flung himself – fearless, furious and bellowing – at our own pure Bella, she tightened her finger on the trigger. Instinctively, protectively, the way one does, she tightened her finger on the trigger.

He screamed when the bullet ripped open the upper part of his left thigh. The momentum of his charge carried him forward, and his body struck hers and they both fell to the ground. The gun skittered into the gutter.

His scream was far louder than his bellow. It was a sharp, high, single-note scream. It didn't rise and fall, like the old woman's wail. And there was a hint of outrage in his scream. A hint of bewildered indignation that such a thing could happen, in a well-ordered society. A hint of disbelief that some woman, some madwoman, some mad, wicked woman, could judge him, and find him guilty, and pump a hard bullet into his soft flesh.

She picked herself up and examined the grazed skin on her hands. She bent for the gun. He'd have to go now. The noise he was making was enough to wake the dead. She'd have to finish him now, before any namby-pamby innocent bystanders came for a look. Not that they would, just for a scream. Shots might bring them, but not a scream. They wouldn't think the shots were really shots. But they'd know the scream. They'd think it was a rape-scream, and a rape-scream doesn't bring anyone.

He was holding his thigh in his hands. He was sobbing with his torn thigh in his hands. She put the barrel against his chin. Then moved it up to his temple. She wanted to be sure. She didn't want to cripple him, to mangle him and leave him still alive. She didn't want her taxes to pay for his treatment for the next fifty years. She held it against his temple.

It was a good way to go. One of the best ways. It was the way she would choose when she had to make the choice. She held her gun to the bitter one's temple, and blasted a bullet into his brain, and banished his bitterness for ever.

This time the bang reverberated. It filled the alley and bounced off the walls and came back at her. The bangs

168

were getting louder. You'd think they'd get quieter, but they were getting louder.

She looked at Mary. Mary looked at her. They looked at each other in the still of the alley. The suddenly quiet and peaceful alley.

The old one shrugged. She might even have smiled. She began to gather her scattered clothes. She pulled all her layers back on again. She covered herself once more with vest and jumpers and coats. She padded out her scrawny form until she became a squat little mushroom that seemed to glide along.

"I'm sorry," Bella said.

"Sorry for what?"

"The noise," she said.

The old one spat.

"If it's not one thing, it's another."

"I know what you mean."

"I only came here for a quiet night."

She regarded her saviour reproachfully.

"Then they came along."

"Can't have been fun."

"Then you came along."

"What can I say?"

The old woman stared at the three young men. She kneeled down beside the bitter one. She passed a hand over his face, and closed his eyes, and picked up the lifeless wrist.

"You off then?" she called to Bella.

"I'm off."

"I'll see you then."

"Okay."

The old one unstrapped the bitter one's watch.

Bella walked back past the quiet one and stepped over the small one and got into the car. She chucked the empty gun out of the window and flicked on the lights. The alley and what she'd done in the alley came into sharp relief. She put the lever into reverse and carefully backed out.

Mary and the bodies slowly shrank. The bodies of the bad boys dwindled in the halogen glare. The car backed into the road. She looked down the alley once more, to fix it in her mind. A frozen winter scene. She wished she'd brought a camera. Mary and her bad boys. Mary and her toy-boys. Mary and her little lambs.

# CHAPTER NINETEEN

She dumped the car on Madeira Drive, near the Dolphin-arium. It must have been four in the morning. Something like that. The first train didn't run till six, which left her a couple of hours to kill. Black night had fallen in Brighton.

She crossed the esplanade and passed the coach departure point and stood in the mouth of the darkened pier, gazing at the Palace of Fun. The arcade was empty. The fairy lights were out. The low-life had gone for the night.

She went down the stone steps by the jetty, and walked past shuttered ice-cream kiosks and souvenir shops. She waded through the take-away tack that littered the path. This is her farewell walk. This is her farewell walk along the shore.

She knew she'd miss it, once she'd gone. Even a beach as dirty as Brighton's beach, and a sea as polluted as Brighton's sea, held their place in her heart. The Thames, the stinking Thames, that finger of slime that fouls its way through London, would be a poor exchange. She hated the capital. All those people, all that noise, all the loonies that lurked about. It didn't seem right that she had to leave. But she had to leave.

The sea sucked and hissed at her side. Ahead and to the left West Pier jutted through a shroud of fog. She crunched along the beach. They tore the guts out of West Pier. They say they had to do it, before it all collapsed. West Pier is her favourite pier. Her all-time favourite pier. It is first among piers, the pier of piers, a peerless pier. You want to troll down to the coast in February. You want to pop down, if you have a moment. You want to see West Pier as it should be seen.

They've stopped cleaning off the mess the gulls drop, and it stands out white against the grey English sea. It's forlorn and desolate and ravaged, and they want to pull it down. They say it's unsafe. They say it's an eyesore. They say it detracts from the rest of the town.

Pygmies and philistines.

It's the town that detracts from the pier. Bella knows these things. Bella has feelings. Bella has an aesthetic sense. She would leave West Pier as a shrine, a place of pilgrimage, a disembowelled and waterlogged house of worship. They should leave it like it is. It takes your breath away like it is. It breaks your heart just like it is.

She walked along the shore. There's no sand on Brighton beach. If you like sand on your beaches, you don't go to Brighton. Brighton's beach is a pebble-strewn beach. You don't walk along Brighton beach, you crunch along, sinking down with each step. If you want to wade through pebbles, you should try wading through Brighton beach. It's like crossing a bog with no mud. You can walk right along where the waves come crashing down. It's a blissful, elemental feeling, if you like that type of thing. Someone closer to nature than she might even have enjoyed it.

She walked along Brighton beach, the best bit of Brighton beach, the bit that went from pier to pier. She was alone on the beach. It was four in the morning, or thereabouts, and she was alone on the beach. She barely realised she was alone. She was barely conscious of being alone. At the end of a February weekend, in the dregs of a Sunday night, in a calf-length skirt and lace-up boots, she walked alone along the beach.

172

The pebbles sucked at her feet, and the sea sobbed at her side, and the bitter wind filled her mouth, and she's come so far and she's climbed so high that being alone doesn't matter any more. Let them see her on the shore. Let them try and touch her on the shore. Let them do it, if they dared.

Bella's at peace with herself and the world. She's done what she did, now she'll try and forget. She finished them all. Foreclosed on their loans. Gave them notice to quit. No longer a lamb on the butcher's block. No longer the lingering fear. She's out on her own, on a moonlit night, and she's striding along by the sea.

She walked on towards the gaunt and gutted West Pier, and with each step she took, with each sucking, crunching, pebble-moving step, she heard another, an echo, a counterpoint to her point. And this was a phenomenon she'd never noticed before. Nature playing tricks again. She walked on, and the echo of her footsteps followed. She stopped, and the echo stopped. She started again, and the echo started. She turned, and saw an empty beach stretching back towards Kemp Town. She walked on towards West Pier, and the staccato sound of a steel-capped boot came beating from above.

They call them monkey-boots, those boots. Feel-small, walk-tall boots. Combat boots. Skinhead boots. Doc Marten boots. Don't-mess-with-me boots.

She stopped and stared up at the prom, and there, by the light of a silvery moon, an anorak hood over his head, taking the air at four in the morning, hands sunk deep in trouser pockets, stood a man, of indeterminate age, though athletic-looking.

She couldn't see his face, which was shadowed by the hood, but she could see he was watching her. There's nothing new under the sun, the Good Book says. Everything is repeated. The circle closes and begins again. Nothing changes. No-one learns. He was watching her. She was out on her own and he was watching her. She stood by the sea

173

and he was watching her. She shivered on the shore and he was watching her.

She pulled up the collar of her thin summer coat. They really shouldn't watch her. She thought they would have known, by now, that they really shouldn't watch her.

She looked up at him in his hood. She could almost feel the filth that clung to him. He wanted to unclean her. He wanted to dirty her with his touch. He wanted to touch her with his dirt. She trembled in the wind as she stood on the shore.

His face was hidden by the hood. He ought to wear a bell. He ought to wear a bell around his neck. He looked like some medieval leper in that hood, and he ought to wear a bell. Then healthy people, undiseased people, people whose skin didn't leak pus, could hear him coming and leave him something on the pavement.

She could have left him a little heap of porno pictures, a lock of pubic hair, or something in rubber he could rub against. That's what they did with lepers, in medieval times. They left food for the afflicted, they gave them what they needed, they let the lepers live their leprous lives, so long as they remembered to wear the bell.

And she wondered what it was that drew them. She wondered why they came like moths and flew into her flame. What urge impelled them, lemming-like, to cross her path. What musky odour she must emit, what scent of rutting promise must invisibly veil her.

But she's not complaining. Don't get her wrong. She's not saying she's had enough. Because, if truth be told, and frankly speaking, she hasn't. She hasn't had enough. She hasn't broken enough bones. She hasn't crushed enough kidneys. She hasn't fired enough bullets, the bliss of firing bullets.

Because once you start, once you really start, you don't really want to stop. You begin to feed an appetite you didn't know you had, and however much you consume, you come to see that it's never enough.

You get that itch. You get that hungry, angry itch and you go for a walk along the shore. You go for a stroll along the shore, and you're hoping a leper will come along. You go for a stroll at four in the morning, because it's your last night in Brighton, and you know what they say about last nights anywhere. It's like the last night of a play, you have to make it good. You go for a walk through the pebbles, and you hope that a leper will be lurking on the prom.

You stand with your back to the white West Pier. You watch him climb down the cold stone steps. You see the nylon anorak. You sense the shadowed face in the leper hood. You wait for him to step off the last stone step and stand on the pebbled beach.

And even though it's what you wanted, you feel an ancient fear. Even though it's what you needed, you feel your nerve begin to go.

Because each time you do this, every single time, it's just you against the leper. And one day the leper will get lucky.

# CHAPTER TWENTY

He stood on the promenade and looked down at her. He saw a dark figure against the white of West Pier. He looked up and down the empty beach, and up and down the empty prom, and he chuckled quietly to himself as he went down the nearest set of stone steps and stood on the pebbled beach. He stood on the pebbles with his hands in his pockets, and stared at a woman who was dark against the white of West Pier.

He stood at the foot of the stone steps and watched her. Her long skirt billowed beneath a thin summer coat. He thought she might be a student. There was something studious about the way she stood there. He'd always wanted to have a student. The skirt would make it easier. The trouble with tight jeans, the basic trouble with jeans that clung tight to the female form, was that although they looked all right, although they looked so good they got you going in the first place, you had to ease them over protesting thighs, which wasn't always easy. But the skirt would definitely make it easier. It was just a case of up and under, with a skirt. Or under and up. He chuckled to himself. He liked himself, very much.

He watched the billowing skirt. He wanted to bury himself in that skirt. He wanted to wrap its folds around him. He wanted to tunnel his way through it to the treasure it concealed. He wanted to push his way inside her. He wanted to force his way inside her. He wanted to bruise her and make her bleed. He wanted to hurt her. He wanted to hurt her badly. He wanted to hurt her madly. He wanted to show her that she really shouldn't walk along the shore.

It wasn't her. Not her as such. Not her, as such, he was going to slash. He didn't hate her, though he tried. He never hated any of them. He never even knew them. He got to know them afterwards. The write-up in the paper. The lives they'd led. The friends they'd had. The things they'd done. He often thought he might have liked to know them better.

They never wrote about the injuries. They were very vague about the injuries. Just as well, it seemed to him. He wouldn't want to read about the way they'd gone. Some things, he used to say, are better left unsaid.

They used to try to talk to him, the ladies did. (He always thought of them as ladies.) They tried to let him know they had a name. He smiled as he remembered. The tricks those ladies tried, as they tried to make him stop.

The screamers were the worst. No self-control. No style. The red mouth open like a sewer. The high-pitched ululations. The shrillness piercing through his brain. It made him mad, the noise they made. He had to shut them up.

The wetters were the best. They wet themselves and thought he wouldn't bother, as if a spot of urine made a difference. Some didn't always mean it when they did it. They did it from their fear of him, the darlings. He liked to watch them wee until they'd emptied. The steamy splashing on the pavement as he looked them in the eye. The shame their fresh young faces showed. He felt a kind of fondness for their weak, distended bladders.

He didn't like the gabbers. They thought that if they talked to him they'd tame him. They must have thought him dense, the things they said. They promised him they'd meet him in the week. They said they'd come and see him in his flat. He'd listen to their lying babble, the words they used to slither out. He'd listen grimly to their gabbing, saying nothing as they spoke. He'd heard it all before, their pleas in mitigation: the periods, the pregnancies, the syphilitic sores. The pointless prattle washed around him as he let them blubber on.

The kickers were the funniest. They'd done some course and thought it would protect them. They kicked his shins with their pointed toes. They jabbed at him with a bunch of keys. They thought they'd send him sprawling down with their evening-class karate. He let them rain their blows on him, their puny little blows. It made him laugh, the way they moved. That woman way. That lumpy, dumpy female way. It made him laugh.

The runners were the brightest. He would have done the same, if he were them. They couldn't get away, but at least they had a go. A woman's hips aren't made for running down a dark, deserted road. He loved his ladies when they ran. Their short and stockinged legs. The sharply panting breaths they took. The whimper when he caught them. The chase and capture warmed him up, which always helped.

He watched his student turn and walk towards the pier. He watched her figure move towards the whiteness of West Pier. She wanted him. He knew she wanted him. He could tell she wanted him, for she turned and walked towards the pier.

He walked behind her, twenty yards behind her, as she moved towards the underbelly of the pier. He watched the way her skirt kept swaying as she walked. He could see her lace-up ankle boots, stepping lightly on the stones. From the skirt and the boots and the flow of her hips he could tell that she wanted him.

He liked to go to the funerals. The gravity always got to him. He tried to make a point of talking to the parents. A brief and sober handshake for the father. A murmured word of comfort for the mother. The self-effacing stepping-back as others came to say their piece. He'd stand bareheaded in the rain and watch his ladies laid to rest: daughters, sisters, sometimes mothers. The polished words, the graveyard grief, the priestly incantations. He often shed a tear or two.

The pebbles scrunched beneath him as he walked towards West Pier. He stepped across the stones as he let her lead the way. He couldn't tell, from the way she moved, what kind she was. Screamer, kicker, gabber, wetter. His groin was warming by the minute. He was good at what he did. They'd have to give him that.

He'd honed his skills. He'd pared them down.

They sometimes said he did it, when he didn't. They said he'd been in Birmingham, on which he wouldn't piss. It must have been some Benny, some stupid, local berk, who took that girl and stuck her like a pig.

They wrote it up in all the rags. It made him mad. He wasn't even well that week. He went out with his temperature and did it there and then. (The lady was a wetter.) He sliced her up the front. They made him do it. They drove him to it. They never should have written what they wrote.

He watched his student step beneath the broken pier. A kicker, from the look of her. To know he came behind her and still go beneath the pier, she'd have to be a kicker, by the look of her.

She stopped and waited. Even had her back to him. She thinks she'll kick me in the crotch, he thought. She wants a fight. She thinks she'll win. He loved it when they had a go. He loved it when they fought him. It made his courage grow.

He came up right behind her, and whispered in her ear. "How much d'you charge, love?"

She turned and lifted up her eyes. She looked much smaller than she'd looked from twenty yards away. She had a wispy, waiflike look. He hadn't thought she'd be so small. It made it simpler, her being so small. Beneath the blackened husk of the remnants of the pier, he felt so big beside her. He looked at her, and felt his courage grow.

179

He saw her face in the light from the sea. She wore no hood. She swathed no silken scarf around her head. She let her hair go streaming in the wind. He looked down at her, the smallness of her, the birdlike, waiflike weakness of her, and felt his courage grow.

"How much d'you charge, love?"

She almost moved her arm. They didn't know how slow they were. He saw her as she almost moved her arm. His hand snaked out.

He'd honed his skills. He'd pared them down.

His hand snaked out and grasped her by the slim and naked neck. He had her by the neck. He had his hand around her neck, and squeezed it very gently. You wouldn't have thought he could squeeze so gently, the big man that he was.

But he's done this many times. He's not a total novice at this game. He's not a greener. No beginner. He's done it once or twice before. He knows you have to squeeze them gently. He knows you have to press them lightly, if you want to make it last.

He watched her choking, gasping, dying, between his fingers. It made his courage grow. He felt so big as he looked down on her, from within the nylon hood. He loved this bit of what he did, this squeezing bit. He also loved the bit that followed. He never knew for sure which bit he loved the more. The squeezing, choking, suffocating bit. Or the biting, thrusting, gouging bit. He loved them both so much it made him ache.

But he never let them die on him. Not by the neck. He never killed them by the neck. He never let them suffocate, which took a rare and Pierrepoint skill. He only squeezed them slightly, gently, tightly, until they sagged, and their legs went limp, and they felt like melted butter in his hands.

He squeezed and felt her nearly choke beneath his fingers. It sent a shudder up his arm, the way it always did. It made him shudder, to feel her choke, beneath his gently pressing fingers.

180

# CHAPTER TWENTY-ONE

"How much d'you charge, love?"

He was bigger than he looked, from twenty yards away. He was Geordie, from his voice. He had a Geordie voice. The Geordie face was blank beneath its leper hood. She couldn't have put a face to the gentle, Geordie voice. He had a scarf around his face, and the hood around his head. He was nobody's fool. He might have been a leper, but he was nobody's fool.

He'd come up right behind her and whispered in her ear. His sibilance in her ear. His soft, Newcastle hiss that kissed her ear. And when she turned and saw how big he was, how surprisingly big he was, she felt the old familiar fear. The fear came up and whispered in her ear.

"How much d'you charge, love?"

She's always liked the Geordie accent. It's her favourite accent, of all the accents. She would have told him, but he shut her up. She tried to move her arm, but didn't know how slow she was. She saw his hand snake out and felt it grip her neck.

He'd honed his skills. He'd pared them down.

She felt his fingers gently press around her neck. She felt them lightly squeezing. Ever so lightly, ever so tightly, she felt them knead the non-existent flesh around her neck. She felt her empty, airless lungs, the black night blacken around her. The faceless leper's hood stared down. He pressed his gentle fingers round her neck, and began to squeeze the life from her not quite lifeless lungs. She felt herself begin to die a slow and stealthy death.

Not yet, she tried to say. I wasn't ready yet. You caught me unawares. Let's start again. I'm only just beginning. You mustn't end me now. One more chance. Just one more chance. Give me one more chance.

She was slipping, falling, plunging. Her legs went limp, her body felt as soft as butter. And then, as if he'd read her mind, she felt his fingers loosen. His fingers loosened on her neck. He had his arms around her. He pulled her to his belly. He pressed his mouth against her head and murmured Geordie mouthings into her fanned-out hair.

"Baby, baby, baby."

She let him hold her weakness to his belly. She felt his courage grow. He held her in his arms and murmured his endearments in her hair. She heard his baby, baby, baby in her very favourite accent. She could have told him, if he'd asked her, if he'd cared to know.

It wasn't right, to finish at West Pier. To finish her weekend beneath West Pier. To do the things she'd done, and all the time her fate was waiting in a hood beneath West Pier.

She couldn't move. She was butter on his belly. He was sobbing in her hair. Baby, baby, baby. He pressed her to his belly. Her face was on his nylon jacket. The zip stuck in her cheek. She was butter, melted butter, in his hands.

"I won't hurt you," he was saying. "I won't give you any pain."

He pressed her face against his chest and cried into her hair.

"You shouldn't walk along the shore."

He kissed her frozen ear.

"You won't feel it when I do it."

He rubbed her throbbing neck.

"But if you feel it, when I do it, let me know."
He held her in his arms. He thought he loved her.
"It's only curiosity."
The sobbing stopped. He calmed himself.
"I like to see what ladies have for breakfast."
She felt so weak. She couldn't move. She waited for her life to flash before her. The sea was churning at her side. He'd kill her soon. She always let them get too close. A fault of hers, she knew. Brighton Bella on the beach. About to die. She couldn't move a muscle.

Just one more chance. One final fling. She'd get it right this time. She felt so weak, but she felt no fear. She had no fear. She conquered fear, and watched it leak away. Drop by fearful drop, her fear began to leak away.

He had no finer feelings. He felt his courage grow, but he didn't feel her fear, as it slowly leaked away. He had no feeling for other people. He couldn't feel what they were feeling. He only felt what he was feeling. He held her with an iron hand, and slipped the other inside her coat. He didn't know what he was risking. He didn't know what he was losing. He didn't know she felt no fear. He couldn't feel what she was feeling, and he slipped one hand inside her coat to try to feel the only thing of hers he thought worth feeling.

He put his hand inside her skirt. He snapped the elastic on her pants. He had his hand inside her summer coat, inside her skirt, and slid his finger up her bone-dry slit. His legs bent out to open hers. He murmured – "Don't be shy, love" – in her ear.

She felt his hand inside her coat begin to feel her. He bunched his fist. The edges of his signet ring pressed sharp against her lips. She knew he'd shove his fist right up inside her. She knew he'd shove his bunched-up fist inside her. She knew that then he'd twist it, and the ring would rip her womb.

He held her with a single hand, and felt her with the other. He held her with his clamp-like grip. He held her fast. But not quite fast enough. So one more chance, one final fling, she hoped she'd get it right this time.

She flicked her flick-knife open. She pressed the button. The blade shot out. She stuck it in his side. She pushed it through the nylon of his nylon anorak, and it went between his ribs and stabbed at something in his side. She stuck it in him. It slashed inside him. It might have been his liver, for all she knew. He held her to his belly, with his fist about to bruise her, and she slashed him very quickly in his side.

He had his hand inside her summer coat, inside her skirt, about to shove his fist right up her shame, when something hot sliced through him from the side. He felt a poker heat cut through his skin. It burnt its way inside him. It might have sliced his liver, for all he knew. He pushed her from him with the hand that held her. He took the hand that had explored inside her summer coat and placed it on his side. He felt a sticky wetness on his fingers. A dark and liquid stain was spreading on his palm. She'd cut him. The bitch had cut him. She'd cut him, even though he'd kissed her hair.

She watched him stare at dark-stained fingers. No light to see the scarlet on those fingers. She could have told him, if he'd asked her, not to put his hand inside her coat. She could have told him that you need both hands to hold a Bella. You need to hold her tight with both your hands, or she'll take her Persian flick-knife and stick it in your side.

It frightened him to see his bloodstained fingers. It made his courage seep away. It made him want to start again. He felt his courage leaving him. Goodbye, it said. Farewell, old chum. Time to say adieu. He had an urge to lick the sticky fingers. He watched his courage gaily walk away.

"Don't go," he cried. "Don't leave me now."

"I won't," she said, and stabbed him once again.

And the stabbing, when she stabbed him, was something rather odd. It wasn't like the bludgeoning of Timbo. It wasn't like the way she'd finished Norman. It wasn't like

184

the mashing up of Reggie. It wasn't like her trigger-happy triumph in the alley.

The stabbing, she discovered, was something strangely intimate. It took a tender touch to place the knife so neatly. To stab him, she discovered, was to know him. You have to get so close to stab. You can't be stand-offish, when you stab. Put your trust in your sword, and the sword in his side. But quickly, cleanly, nothing nasty. You jab-jab here, you stab-stab there. You put it in. You take it out. You put it in again.

He felt the knife go in and out. He felt her knife inside him. He didn't know a knife could hurt so much. He would have wept, if he'd had the strength. It wasn't right, what she had done. It wasn't fair. If he'd have known she had a blade, he would have been prepared. He would have slit her open straight away. She should have said. The scrubber should have said. She hadn't played the game. To think he'd thought she was a lady. He felt the knife go in and out.

She had to do it quickly now. The thing about the knife, the thing you must remember, if you think you'd like a knife: it's only as strong as the hand that holds it. And if the hand isn't strong, it must be quick. She has to quickly slide it in him, here, there and everywhere. She has to slash him where she can, before he reaches out and takes the wrist that bears the hand that holds the knife, and snaps it like a twig.

The urgency with which she stabbed him was impressive to behold. She really got stuck in. And with each jab a soft and guarded grunt came from her parted lips. She grunted as she stabbed him, but softly, like a lady. And with each jab he grunted in reply. They grunted back and forth. They sounded like a courting couple, grunting in the shadows of the pier.

The frenzy of it, the lunging, plunging madness of it, really took it out of her. It's physical and tiring work. He just kept standing there. He oozed and spurted like a plum. She hasn't struck the fatal blow, the mortal, lethal, fatal blow that'll put him on the ground. The big man that he was, she had to knife him endlessly. She slashes upwards with the blade. She cuts the scarf around his skin. She stabs the knife beneath his hood and opens up his face. He staggers, but – perversely – doesn't fall.

"I'll tell you something funny," she says, pausing for a well-earned breather, "I really liked your voice."

She took the hilt in both her hands. She heaved with all her might. She shoved the blade right in his chest, his beating core, his throbbing heart of darkness, not to coin a phrase.

He took her hands in both of his. It was a touching scene. His heart was pumping through the steel. The blade vibrated with the beat. The pulse of him grew faint. His leprous breath blew in her face one last and loathsome time. She thought she heard him say his name was Jack.

He spurted in the way she made men spurt. He gushed all over her, without restraint. He blooded her and then he fell. She watched him sink down to his knees. The sea-light lit his leper's face. He looked perplexed. She wanted to explain, to tell him why, to let him know why he had to go. She saw him pull the knife out from his chest, and try to stand, and heard him sigh, and watched him fall below the surf.

He rotated in the waves. They spun him round. They made him bob and weave. She watched him float face down, and wished that he would sink. He ebbed and flowed before her, a piece of Geordie flotsam. They'd say another body was washed up on Brighton beach. She'd always wondered where they came from, and now she supposed she knew.

He'd bled all over her summer coat. She'd have to leave it on the shore. The messiness, the mess of it, she never would get used to.

He could have guessed, he should have known. She could have told him, if he'd asked her. She could have told him not to bother. She could have said it loud and clear. She could have whispered in his ear:

If you see a woman walking, if she's stepping quietly home, if you see her flowing past you on the pavement. If you'd like to break her brittle bones, and you want to hear the hopeless pleading, and you want to feel the pink flesh bruising, and you want to taste the taut skin bleeding.

If, in fact, you see her and you want her.

Think on. Don't touch her. Just let her pass you by. Don't place your palm across her mouth and drag her to the ground.

For unknowingly, unthinkingly, unwittingly you might have laid your heavy hand on Bella. And she's woken up this morning with the knowledge that she's finally had enough.